LOVELY

Autumn J. Bright

A
LIGHT
BULB
Publishing

North Carolina

Library of Congress Control Number: 2017910755

ISBN: 978-0-9861923-4-0

Printed in the United States of America

First Edition

Cover design by Damonza
Photography by Jennifer Wolfe

www.autumnjbright.com

www.alightbulbpublishing.com

Dedicated to all the Lovelies of the world…live

&

In memory of Dr. George L. Brown

We come to this world just a clump of clay ready to be molded.

LOVELY

Prologue

IN the dead of an October night, a knock on the front door caused Dolores Duval to jump out of her sleep. "Joseph!" she whispered urgently while shaking her husband's arm. "Get up. Someone's at the door."

"What?" he responded, barely awake.

"Someone's at the door," she repeated louder.

Joseph turned and gave his tired eyes a squint to focus on the clock. He looked at his wife again. "Dolores, do you know what time it is? It's almost two o'clock in the morning. Ain't nobody out there. You probably just heard the wind knocking up against the porch. Now, please, honey, go back to sleep."

"Joseph, you go back to sleep," she snapped then reached for her housecoat draped over the chair. "I'm telling you I heard something, and I'm going to see what it is."

"Now, just hold on a minute," Joseph said, raising his voice a little. He rubbed his eyes then snatched his glasses off the nightstand. "There's no need to get snippy and bent out of shape about it. Just give me a second to put on my slippers. I'm coming."

The middle-aged couple approached the front door with caution and opened it to find a note wedged between the screen door.

"What is it, Mama?" Irene asked, walking up from behind them. "Who's at the door?"

They suddenly heard a cry. Dolores gasped and pushed the door wider. And there on the porch, on a cool night, lay a baby all bundled up in a worn-out plastic laundry basket.

"Lord, have mercy!" Dolores shouted with wide terrified eyes. She grabbed the baby and started rocking it in her arms. "Who in the world would leave an infant on the porch like this?" Dolores peered into the darkness.

Irene picked the note off the ground. Her face went pale. "Mama," she said, rolling her eyes at the paper. "It's from Corinne."

The look of disappointment washed over Dolores' face. It all seemed too familiar. She let out an exhausted sigh. "Well, go ahead and read it."

Irene paused for a few moments, preparing her nerves for the load of crap she was about to read out loud.

Dear Duval Family,

I don't know what to say. I guess I messed up again. After all these years, it seems I still can't get it together. I just can't handle children right now. Please give Lovely the same upbringing and love you've given Cynthia. They deserve so much...much more than I could ever give them. I hope you can forgive me.

Forever grateful,
Corinne
P.S.... I'm sorry, Irene.

Irene crushed the letter in her hand. She felt a surge of emotions running through her body: anger, hurt, and betrayal. But mainly shock. They were all shocked. It had been five years since they'd seen or heard from Corinne, five years since Corinne begged Irene back in college while they were sophomore roommates to help with the first pregnancy. And it had been five long years since she broke her promise to be a part of Cynthia's life. Now, Corinne was back with the audacity to dump yet another child on their laps.

"Mama, we don't have to do this," Irene declared as she flipped through phone book pages. "We don't always have to save Corinne when she's in trouble. We need to call her family or social services. Who does she think we are—an orphanage?" She shook her head as she moved next to the phone. "Oh, no, she is not going to take advantage of us again. I'm tired of her."

"Now, wait a minute, Irene. Let's just think about this before you make any phone calls," Joseph said as he sat on the couch next to his daughter. He took the phone out of her hand and hung it up.

"We all know Corinne is wrong," Joseph continued. "The first time, it was an accident. The second time, well, there's no excuse. But, we also know that family of hers isn't going to take this child in. We've already been down this road before."

Irene blew out a long sigh, knowing her father was right. She remembered how Corinne's parents were so strict and religious about almost everything. But, most of all, she remembered how they never gave one objection to Cynthia's adoption at the courthouse and still refused to be involved in any aspect of her life today. "Children born out of wedlock are bastard children and seedlings of the devil," Irene once heard Corinne's mother say.

"Listen, Dolores," Joseph said, "we encouraged your sister to adopt Cynthia because she couldn't have any babies of her own. And now that Richard and Harriet are going through some tough times, there's no way they can afford another mouth to feed. So, I think we should adopt Lovely for ourselves. My point is this: She's got an older sister right across the street; it would be wrong of us to separate these girls. When you put everything else aside, y'all know I'm right."

Dolores stared at the baby. *Just a crying shame,* she thought. The child had been on the earth for only a blink of an eye and was already facing problems that were none of her doing. And in that moment, the decision was made. The little girl would be raised as their own. Lovely was family.

Part I

Chapter 1

IT was just my luck! On the last day of school, I had to be sitting right smack in front of Winston Elementary's worst gang of misfits. The school bus couldn't get me home fast enough. Tasha Brown and her dim-witted friends were at it again, shooting nasty spitballs through straws at the back of my freshly pressed hair. Who knew stopping to say goodbye to my favorite teachers would land me a seat among a firing squad?

"Stop it Tasha! Stop it," I turned around and screamed. "If you don't stop it, I'll—"

"You'll what, Lovely? Tell your mama?" Tasha said with an attitude, shifting her neck from left to right and standing way too close to me.

And on cue, the kids at the back of the bus started *oohing* and laughing.

"But, oh, that's right," she continued loudly, smacking on a big wad of chewing gum. "You ain't got no mama. You were left on the porch by a stork in the middle of the night."

Everyone within earshot started laughing. This was my last day being a student at Winston Elementary. In the fall, I would be starting middle school and leaving Tasha behind, yet again,

in the fourth grade. I got fed up with all her teasing and
bullying over the years. This time she had it coming.

"Why don't you shut up you stupid, fat cow!" I yelled,
shoving Tasha's bubble butt back into her seat. "I bet you
can't even spell stork."

"Fight! Fight! Fight!" the kids egged on in chorus.

I wasn't sure I could give Tasha a good beatdown, but I
gave my eyes a squint, put my deuces up anyway, and hoped
for the best.

"Shut that noise up!" Ms. Gaston, the bus driver, hollered.
"There will be no fighting on my bus today. Do y'all want me
to pull over?"

Nobody wanted Ms. Gaston to stop the bus. She was like
a mama and a daddy all rolled into one and had a goatee and
mustache to prove it. And when she got to fussing, her voice
was like a boom box and you could see all of her missing teeth.
Only those pointy canines remained.

"Tasha, sit your tail down," she continued to regulate from
the oversized rear view mirror.

"But I didn't do anything," Tasha hissed. "Lovely pushed
me down."

Ms. Gaston hit the brakes and gave her famous *don't play
with me* look.

"Yes, ma'am." Tasha quickly followed orders, folding her
arms over, pouting and flaring her nostrils. The girl sitting next
to Tasha gave her a slight smile.

"What are you gawking at?" Tasha snapped.

"Now, Lovely, come up here and sit behind me. Sit next
to Jamal."

As I walked toward the front of the bus, I could hear Tasha mumble, "Imma getcha good, Lovely" under her breath. But I wasn't afraid. Tasha lived too far away from my house to walk. Besides, that would be like exercise. And C.C. Johnson Middle School was about a twenty-five minute drive from Winston Elementary. I figured by the time Tasha graduated to middle school, I would be in high school. So, I ignored her stupid little threat.

I sat down next to Jamal as instructed. He was the new kid on the block, a fifth grader who lived three houses down from me. Rumor had it his father was serving a long-term jail sentence in upstate South Carolina for armed robbery, leaving Jamal, his mom, and younger sister behind to fend for themselves and rent out the old Curtis house.

"Hi," he said, with a small smile.

Oh, wow! Sirens went off in my head. In all of the eight months of Jamal living in the neighborhood and us sharing the same bus stop, this was the first time he'd ever said anything to me. It didn't bother me he never spoke when I'd smile at him at the bus stop. I just figured he was the quiet-shy type who was too afraid to look people in the eyes or he wasn't raised with good manners.

"Hey," I replied, returning the same small smile.

"That was a pretty brave thing you did back there," he said. "Not too many people stand up to Tasha the way you did and keep their two front teeth." Jamal chuckled.

"Yeah, I'm not worried about Tasha," I said, rolling my eyes. "She's just a big ole dumb bully."

Jamal shook his head and flashed a bigger grin.

"You know, Jamal," I said with one eyebrow raised, "I think she's jealous of me. I can read and write and get good grades in school with no problems. But she's not too swift and has to repeat the same grade almost every year. Must be frustrating being twelve years old and still in elementary school." I turned and looked Jamal's way. "Don't you think?"

Jamal nodded as we smiled hard at each other. Then it began. He started up with that daggone giggling, and I followed right behind him. His giggles were so contagious, we had to cup our mouths with our hands and lean over into the seat so no one could hear or see our laughter. We couldn't stop and laughed until we cried and our stomachs ached.

"You're funny, Lovely." Jamal caught his breath to speak. "And I like your name too."

"Thanks," I managed to get out.

As I recovered from laughing my brains out, I started to wonder if Jamal was going to C.C. Johnson in the fall. He seemed like a cool person. And to be honest, already having a friend at a brand new school would be a great relief.

"So, what about you?" I asked. "Did you pass? Are you going to middle school next year?"

"Yeah, I'm going to the sixth grade next year."

"Well, good," I said. "That's something we have in common. Maybe now we can speak to each other at the bus stop sometimes?"

Jamal nodded while pushing his drooping glasses up his nose.

"All right, Lovely, here's your stop," Ms. Gaston announced warmly. "Tell ya mama I said hello and you take care of yourself in school next year, ya hear?"

"Yes ma'am," I replied.

As the bus rolled away, I could see Tasha in the window waving her middle finger at me. She was like an irritating thorn I just plucked out of my big toe after running barefoot through an open field in the summer. I stuck my tongue out at her then looked over at Jamal. We burst into loud laughter again. Soon, the yellow elementary bus and Tasha Brown became distant images on the road.

Chapter 2

LIKE clockwork, Mama was sitting on the front porch waiting for me to return home from school. And, as usual, her long salt and pepper hair was neatly tucked into a bun, and she had on one of her numerous oversized muumuus she loved to put on for cooking. Normally, Mama wore simple clothes and stayed away from anything flashy, but for some reason, she really enjoyed those multicolored muumuu dresses. The busier the pattern, the more she seemed to like it.

The year was 1984 and as long as I'd known her, Mama had always been predictable. So predictable you could set your watch by her daily routine during the school week.

Breakfast: 7:30 AM
Mama sitting on the porch: 2:45 PM
Dinner on the table: 6:00 PM

The weekends and special times were no different. We went to church every Sunday and sat in the same spot and Mama always had freshly baked chocolate chip cookies ready for me on the last day of school. These days, at sixty-five, Mama enjoyed being a retired librarian and a predictable homemaker.

"Who was that handsome boy you were walking with, Lovely?" she asked, smiling as I walked up the driveway.

"Oh, that's Jamal Turner. You know the family that moved into Mr. Curtis' old house several months ago."

"Oh, yes," she recalled. "That's that woman whose husband went to jail for stealing."

I was sure Mama got that piece of information from Mt. Moriah Baptist church, which happened to be the place where most of the town's gossip circulated. Mama never started gossip, but she definitely listened to it.

I shrugged. "I guess so."

I never really paid any attention to rumors, especially since I had been the subject of gossip ever since the day I was born. My family never lied to me about my adoption. Knowing how I came into this world gave me a tough skin at an early age.

"Such a shame that poor woman has to raise those kids on her own," Mama continued, still going on about the Turners. "What a pity…"

"Look, Mama, I made the honor roll again!" I blurted, waving my report card in the air, hoping to change the subject. Mama didn't often judge people aloud, but she firmly believed that all children should have a mother and a father at home. There was one problem: When she started talking about something that bugged her, she could go on and on.

"Oh, that's good, baby!" Mama hugged me and kissed my forehead. "I'm so proud of you. C'mon, let's go inside and get you some cookies." The smell of warm chocolate and tonight's dinner hit me the moment the door swung open.

"Did your friend pass as well?" Mama went on to ask.

"Yes ma'am," I answered, walking behind her. "He's going to the sixth grade too."

"Good, now you'll have someone your own age to talk to around here instead of you just clinging to Irene or reading in your bedroom all the time."

Mama had a point. I loved to read and could do it all day. Books took me to places that were fun and interesting. Not like around here in Willisburg, South Carolina—population 3,000. We lived out in the boonies among a few spaced-out houses on a country back road where a bunch of old people live. The only entertainment I got was from reading or catching fireflies in the yard during the summers. And when I really got bored, I'd just hang out with Irene.

"I really think you should try to make some friends at school next year. Maybe some girlfriends," Mama said. "You're growing up, Lovely, and you need to start developing some type of social life, but I think that boy Jamal will do you some good for now."

"Who's Jamal?" Irene asked, sitting in the kitchen eating my cookies.

"What are you doing here?" I asked instead. "I thought you were at work."

"I got off early. And don't change the subject, missy. Who's Jamal? Is that your boyfriend?" she asked with raised eyebrows and a smirk on her face.

"No, Irene!" I wrinkled my nose at her like there was something funky in the air. "He's just a boy who lives down the street."

"Okay, okay. I'm just asking," she said. "Anyway, I like your outfit. You look cute today."

I twirled around to show off my pink and black polka dot dress with black jelly shoes. Anything that had pink or red in it I liked. Those were my favorite colors. They looked good up against my dark skin—at least that's what Mama told me.

"Lovely, what are those white things in your hair?" Irene asked, interrupting my fashion show. "Girl, what were you doing today?" Irene brushed off the back of my dress. "Go look at yourself in the mirror."

Just when I thought I got rid of crazy Tasha, flashbacks from this afternoon came back to haunt me. "Don't even ask," I said, letting out a long sigh while walking away.

I stood in the bathroom mirror and shook spitballs out of my Shirley Temple curls. Mama always did a good job on my hair and kept it healthy and long, just like hers. She said the secret was a mixture of Dax grease, Shea butter, and love. Whatever she used made me the envy of most girls at school and church. Maybe that's the reason I didn't have any female friends—well, except for Anika Douglas. Anika and I had been friends for as long as I could remember. We didn't go to school together, but we saw each other every Sunday at church. And she never seemed interested in my hair. Anika always kept hers in braids.

As I continued to fix myself up, I started to daydream about the upcoming school year. I felt excited because everything would be fresh and new: the school, the teachers, and now Jamal. It was just a couple of months until my new adventure began. I had a good feeling about C.C. Johnson Middle School.

Chapter 3

LATER that evening, Mama made a big dinner in my honor: rice, potato salad, collard greens, fried pork chops, barbeque chicken, macaroni and cheese, cornbread, and sweet tea to wash it all down. When Mama cooked, the scent had a way of traveling outside to hypnotize people and lead them right back to our kitchen. It was like every fifteen minutes I heard the screen door slam shut from folks coming in and then going out with take-out trays.

Smack! I heard once again. This time it was Aunt Harriet walking in to take her turn.

"Dolores, what did you cook?" she yelled from the living room. Aunt Harriet also knew how to roll-a-pot, as the grown-ups would say, but ever since Uncle Richard died four years earlier, she hadn't been doing much cooking at all. Sometimes Aunt Harriet and Cynthia would come by and eat with us. Sometimes Mama would just send me across the street with plates of food.

"We're in the den, Harriet," Mama shouted back.

The long foldout table draped with red plastic was now surrounded by the usual people: Mama, Daddy, Irene, Aunt Harriet, Cynthia, and my eldest sister, Addie, along with her sickening daughter, Deidra. We also had some other people over I recognized from church who I originally thought stopped by to talk to Mama about the pastor's anniversary luncheon next month but decided to stick around to get their fill. I guess Mama expected the large turnout, because she cooked enough food to go around the table about ten times.

"Congratulations, Lovely! My baby is going to middle school," Mama said from the other end of the table. She raised a red plastic cup in the air. Everybody nodded or repeated "Congratulations"…but not Deidra.

"Yes, our baby girl is no longer a baby. She's growing up on us fast, isn't she?" Daddy said with bits of fish hanging from his lips. "Soon she'll be off to college."

The thought of going to college excited me the most. I'd be the next Duval in line to get a college education. Mama went to a two-year college, Daddy went to a vocational school for car mechanics, and both my sisters had bachelor's degrees. But Irene—she actually had a master's degree in education and taught history at Willisburg High School.

Forget Wonder Woman…Irene was my hero. I planned to be a teacher just like her when I grew up. So I'd been reading a lot and keeping my grades up for that very reason.

"I guess it's just going to be you and me, Dolores."

Daddy cracked a smile at me while still eating. This time he managed to get food on his cheek and on the bottom rim of his glasses. Funny thing though, there was more food on his face than on that napkin he had dangling from his collar.

"Oh my goodness." Addie laughed as she passed paper towels down the table. "Daddy, please, clean your face. You've got food all over you."

"Well, this is what happens to ya when you get old and your hand shakes. Sometimes you miss the hole."

Daddy laughed then continued to aim food at his mouth. Even with Parkinson's disease, he still had a sense of humor and a strong will to do whatever he wanted.

With all this talk about me going away for college, a couple questions popped up in my mind. *How can I abandon my parents for college in their old age? And who will take care of them when I'm gone?*

"Daddy, I'm never gonna leave you and Mama," I blurted. "That's why I'm going to a local college after high school—so I can watch over you two."

Daddy wiped his mouth. "Oh, honey, you don't have to worry about us. You need to choose a school that's going to give you the best education. And that may take you away from us. Besides, going away for college is just part of the whole experience. You'll get your degree, a good job, and then one day, you'll get married and have a family of your own."

"Now that's for sure," one of the church ladies said from the end of the table. "A pretty girl like you won't have any trouble finding a husband." And just when she said that, I saw Deidra cut her eyes and press her lips together. I don't know why, but that niece of mine had never liked me from day one. Even when Deidra was at Winston elementary, she never helped with the bullies even though she was two years older than me. Irene told me not to pay her any mind because she was moody just like her mama.

"I think Lovely may already have a suitor in waiting," Irene said, flashing that same goofy expression she gave me earlier.

"Ooh, does Lovely have a boyfriend?" Cynthia teased as she made faces at me as well from across the table.

"Who are you talking about, Irene?" Aunt Harriet asked.

"I'm talking about the boy who walked Lovely home today," Irene answered then looked at me. "His name is Jamal. Isn't that right, Lovely?"

I couldn't believe she mentioned Jamal in front of everybody. I was so embarrassed. "Yes, that's his name. And no, he didn't walk me home." I rattled off with my eyes bugged out, making sure Irene saw my disapproval. "We go to the same bus stop, that's all. He's not my boyfriend!"

"That's the boy who lives down the street, right Dolores?" Aunt Harriet began to investigate. "He belongs to that woman who's renting out Curtis' old house, right?"

"Well, I heard she really isn't renting it," one of the church ladies said.

"Lorraine, what do you mean she's not really renting the house?" Mama asked, chuckling.

"Well, that's what I heard, Dolores. I was told that family is on some kind of housing program where the government moves people out of the city projects, puts 'em in the suburbs, and then pays their rent for them. It's supposed to help kids get a better education. But it's also guaranteed money for homeowners—you know what I mean."

Mama grinned and shook her head. "Lorraine, I do believe you missed your calling. You should have been a reporter."

"I do have my sources." Ms. Lorraine dabbed her lips with a napkin.

Addie laughed. "Shoot. I wish the government would pay my rent so I don't have to be trapped in a mortgage."

"Oh, no you don't," Daddy said. "That kind of business comes with too many stipulations. Trust me when I say you don't want the government dictating how much you can earn just to stay in a poor house for free. If you're blessed enough to do it, homeownership is the best way to go."

"Well, I don't care where the boy comes from or who pays his mama's rent," Aunt Harriet continued. "I just hope the fruit falls far...far away from the tree, because I heard that boy's daddy is a thief. You better watch 'em, Lovely."

In my head, I rolled my eyes a thousand times. *Who cares about his father or how the Turners live?* Jamal seemed like an honest person to me.

"Oh, give the boy a break." Mama jumped in...just in time to throw a dose of reasoning in the room. "After all, he's only a child and not responsible for what his father did. Lovely"—she turned to me—"why don't you take some of those leftover cookies to Jamal's house tomorrow and tell his mother I said welcome to the neighborhood?"

"And make sure you invite them to church too," Ms. Lorraine added. "You know, I haven't seen them at church yet."

"Yes ma'am," I replied. Packing up cookies turned out to be the perfect excuse to leave the table and gossip behind. I was born hating gossip.

Chapter 4

IT was late in the afternoon by the time I got the chance to deliver those cookies to the Turners. I spent most of the morning hours cleaning up the yard and picking vegetables from the garden with Mama. The first Saturday in June was sunny and warm—not one cloud in the sky above. It felt like the perfect day for bike riding.

After washing up, I put on my blue jeans, red shirt, and white converse sneakers to match my favorite red bicycle, which I shamelessly plastered with Strawberry Shortcake stickers. My parents gave me the bike as a birthday gift only two years ago but, sadly, I noticed I was beginning to outgrow it back in the fall. I shrugged my shoulders and hopped on anyway. So what my knees almost touched the handle bar when I sat down? I figured this would be my last summer to ride it before Mama would intervene and make me give it up for good.

After unloading my front basket, I walked up to Jamal's front door and knocked.

"Coming," I heard a woman yell. The door opened wide and there stood the prettiest lady I had ever seen.

This is Jamal's mother?

"Hi, my name is Lovely. Are you Jamal's mom?"

"Yes," she answered with a puzzled smile.

I stretched out my arm and gave her the bag of cookies. "This is from me and my mom. We live down the street—welcome to the neighborhood."

"Oh, thank you," she said warmly. "Lovely? Now, that is a unique name. But I see why they call you that. You are absolutely adorable."

"Thank you," I replied, showing her my best picture-perfect smile.

Mrs. Turner was nothing like I imagined. I thought she'd be average looking like most mothers I know...big or just plain looking. But Mrs. Turner was none of those things, and she definitely didn't seem like the muumuu type. She reminded me of Willona Woods from the television show *Good Times*— someone who didn't have a lot of money but still managed to look like a million bucks. She wore her medium-length black hair in a feathered haircut, her makeup sat perfectly on her caramel skin, and her stylish clothes were sharply ironed, like she used the entire can of starch.

She cleared the way and motioned me to come in. "So you and Jamal are friends?"

"Yes ma'am."

Looking around the house, I noticed that Mrs. Turner kept her home just as neat and clean as she was. Everything had its place. The outside of the house may have been worn out and in desperate need of some fresh paint, but inside—the carpet, the kitchen, and all the furniture seemed brand new.

"Jamal!" she shouted down the hallway and then returned her attention to the large gold-colored framed mirror on the wall. "Lovely's out here to see you."

As she continued to fidget with her face and put on door knocker earrings, I noticed she didn't have on a wedding ring. *She's not married?*

"Lovely, you don't have to stand there and watch me beat my face," she joked. "You can have a seat."

I waited another minute or two before Jamal finally came out. He seemed surprised to see me. But who could blame him? It's not like I asked to come here yesterday. "Hey, my mom baked some chocolate chip cookies. She thought you and your family would like a batch."

Jamal's face lit up as he grabbed the bag off the living room table. Somewhere in between opening the bag and devouring two cookies in two breaths, he mentioned chocolate chip was his favorite.

"Hey, boy," his mother snapped. "Save some for your sister."

Jamal chuckled with a mouth full of cookies, which made his cheeks big like a chipmunk's storing nuts for the winter. *Shoot.* If I'd known he'd react like that to Mama's baking, I would have brought more.

Beep. Beep. A car honked.

"That's for me," Mrs. Turner announced. She picked up her purse and then took a final look in the mirror. "Jamal, dinner is in the refrigerator. You know how to warm it up and make sure you share some of those cookies with Nicole."

Mrs. Turner kissed the top of Jamal's head on her way out. "Lovely, it was nice meeting you. And tell your mother Gwen said thanks."

I nodded and waved goodbye.

Impressive for a boy, I thought, returning my attention to Jamal. He was only eleven years old and already knew how to cook and take care of his five-year-old sister.

"Thanks, Lovely." He continued to chomp. "These are so good." Jamal kept scarfing down cookies one after the other. Apparently, he had no intentions of following his mother's orders about sharing.

"So, you have to babysit."

"Yeah, my mom got tickets to see some band called Maze in Charleston. She won't be back until later tonight." Jamal finally pulled out one last cookie then placed the almost empty bag on the kitchen counter.

"You're not scared of being out here alone by yourself at night?" I asked.

Jamal sucked his teeth. "Heck, no! We come from the city projects. In the city, there's a lot of noise and sometimes you've got to dodge the drug man or stray bullets on your way to school. So what's so scary about being out here alone...the woods?"

Jamal let out a hearty laugh then tossed back the last cookie.

His laughter got on my nerves. And so did that tall tale about dodging bullets. An idea sprouted in my head. I knew exactly what to say to wipe that smug look off his face and make him shake in his city boots.

"Well, did you know Mr. Curtis—the old man who used to own this house?"

"No."

"Well, they found him dead—right here in this very living room."

"Oh yeah?"

"Yeah." I bounced my head. "And did you know that there are ghosts out there in those woods?"

"Ha—still not scared." He mocked my attempt to shock him.

I rolled my eyes. Jamal could make fun all he wanted, but I was born here. And I knew those woods could get pretty darn spooky at night. I remembered hearing grown-ups tell creepy stories about the ghosts of enslaved Africans watching over our lands and the Indians who were murdered centuries ago by English settlers and then supposedly had their bodies buried a couple of miles down the road next to the old Smithfield Cemetery. Some say the souls of those same Indians still haunt the woods today. And that's why I stayed clear away from those woods at night.

"Anyway, what are you doing today besides delivering cookies and trying to scare the daylights out of me?" he asked, brushing crumbs off his *Annie* T-shirt.

Annie! I thought, surprised. Jamal seemed more like the nerdy *Star Trek* type rather than a fan of musicals, especially with those bottom-up shirts and khaki pants he normally wore at school.

"Do you have a bicycle?" I asked, taking my focus off his shirt.

"Yeah. Why?"

"Well, I was hoping we could go bike riding, but I see you're busy."

"Yeah, I can't," he said, sounding disappointed. "Maybe some other time?"

I nodded and made my way to the front door to leave. "Oh, I almost forgot. You and your family are invited to visit my church tomorrow. Are you Baptist or Methodist?"

Jamal looked confused.

"Oh, I only ask because my church is Baptist, so be prepared for a whole lot of hollering."

"Well, actually, we're neither," he answered. "We rarely go to church."

Rarely go to church! I balked.

That would cause a riot with Ms. Lorraine and her crew. Church attendance around here was like a mandatory thing.

"Okay." I shrugged, not wanting to make things any more awkward. "But if y'all ever want to come, my church is Mt. Moriah. It's the white building across from Cliff's Auto Parts off of Main Street."

It didn't bother me that the Turners weren't religious people. Deidra went to church every Sunday, and I swear that girl was the devil in the flesh. Who was I to judge? Besides, I knew there were plenty of people around here who'd already do the judging for me.

Chapter 5

ANIKA really did it this time. I watched her head bob back and forth during the entire sermon from the other side of the church. Usually she'd have her hair braided in some fancy pattern. But today, her long braids were shifted into a side ponytail with multi-colored beads decorating each strand. There were so many beads: green, white, and gold to match her green and white summer dress. And you could tell Anika was extra proud of her hairstyle this Sunday morning, because she swung that ponytail at every opportunity she could get. The choir sang a song—she swung. The preacher said make some joyful noise—she swung.

"Anika," I called out over the crowd as church dispersed. As we walked toward each other, we got swept up by a group of fat women. "Are you excited about going to Wando Middle school this fall?" I managed to ask through gaps of oversized breast and stomachs. We ended up outside at the bottom of the steps to talk.

County lines kept Anika and me from going to the same schools. I used to wish we could go to the same schools, but she lived in Charleston County and the long distance commute would be too much for a daily drive. Anika and her mother only came this way once a week to visit family and attend church.

"Am I excited about middle school?" she asked with a sarcastic tone while looking me up and down. "I should be asking you if you're excited about Jamal…your new boyfriend."

"Who told you that?" I demanded, feeling caught off guard.

"Deidra, of course," Anika reported, wearing a silly grin.

"Oh my gosh!" I shrieked.

I scanned the church grounds looking for my no good, rumor-starting niece to give her a piece of my mind—no luck. Just like a rat that just stole cheese, she was nowhere to be found.

"You know you can't believe a word she says, right? She hates me."

Anika laughed. "I know. I just wanted to see your reaction. So who's Jamal anyway?"

I told Anika everything about Jamal…where he lives, how we met, and how that stupid rumor got started. Although Anika was kinda strange, she was the closest thing I had to a best friend. And if I did like Jamal, which I didn't, I surely would have told her.

"Listen, don't pay Deidra any attention by jumping in her face," Anika advised, placing a hand on my shoulder. "Ignore her. She's probably just jealous of you."

"Why would she be jealous of me?" I asked, baffled.

Anika sighed and folded her arms over. "Oh my goodness, Lovely! You know that girl has jealousy issues. Haven't you ever noticed how Deidra only gets an attitude with people who look better than her or do something better than her?"

My mind instantly went back to the other night when Deidra rolled her eyes at me after Ms. Lorraine called me pretty.

"Lovely, she's even jealous of me. I've seen the faces she makes when I sing at church."

I still couldn't fully understand why Deidra would be so jealous of me. She had nice hair and wasn't bad-looking. But Anika's talent was another story.

Anika had a powerful singing voice, the kind of voice that could get you on *Star Search* or a national recording deal. Some folks even said she sounded better than Stacy Lattisaw. Anika performed at church, school plays, Christmas parades, and on occasions—even weddings. It truly amazed people to see a big talent with such great stage presence come from a small ten-year-old body, but showbiz would have to wait. According to Anika, some local promoter gave her an invitation to be the opening act at the New Edition concert, but Mrs. Douglas wasn't having it and turned them down flat. Anika said her mother wanted her to a have a childhood and graduate from high school before pursuing a singing career seriously.

"I think you're right." I smiled. "Deidra is just a jealous person and that's that."

"Lovely," Irene hollered, "it's time to go."

I gave Anika a hug and then ran to the car. "By the way, I like your beads," I shouted, leaning out the window as the car pulled away. I left Anika standing there smiling hard and playing with that darn ponytail.

Chapter 6

"HURRY up! Run faster," I looked back and shouted. "We're going to miss them."

Jamal shifted the straps on his shoulders to help pick up speed. "I'm trying, Lovely." His voice sounded winded. "But this bag is heavy. You could of carried some of this stuff, you know."

Dawn was almost here. And for the third year in the row, Irene invited me to Edisto Beach to watch baby loggerhead sea turtles hatch from nests underneath the sand and then race for their lives to reach the waves before being eaten.

Many years ago, Irene's ex-boyfriend introduced her to this place. He'd brought her here to this very spot as a birthday surprise. Her two-timing boyfriend was long gone now, but she'd been returning to witness this event ever since then. Irene said there's a lesson to be learned in the sea turtle's struggle for survival: *Life can be hard and filled with obstacles, but if you press on, you can reach any goal.*

"You kids remember the rule," Irene shouted from behind us. "Y'all can watch, but leave them be."

My eyes became wide the moment I topped a sand dune and scanned the beach below. There were already dozens—maybe even hundreds—of turtles emerging from holes and waddling across the sand with ghost crabs crawling around and birds squawking overhead.

Irene really has a knack for guessing hatching time.

Using my trusty flashlight, I made sure to watch my step looking for a good place to spread out a blanket. I used my bare feet to gently kick up the cool sand to make sure the spot was clear. And then, from a safe distance, we sat down and watched the turtles as the horizon light rose over the ocean. It was beautiful.

"Are you watching this, Jamal?" I asked. "Isn't this great? I mean, I know it looks kinda gross—the way the turtles just come out of the earth all at once. You know, the first time I saw this, it seemed like the ground was throwing up or something. But still, isn't it awesome?"

"Yeah, but a lot of them aren't going to make it, right? Isn't that what you told me?" he asked, twisting his mouth into a grimace.

"I guess so." I shrugged, watching a group of turtles getting taken out to sea. "But like Daddy always says, that's just the cycle of life."

I turned to Jamal to get his reaction. His eyebrows and forehead were still wrinkled as he continued to look mesmerized by the sight.

Jamal and I had been spending a lot of time with each other ever since school let out for summer break. There wasn't a day in June where we didn't talk over the phone, go bike riding, or explore the woods. Now it was June 30. I practically begged Irene to let Jamal tag along this morning.

"Jamal, is this your first time seeing turtles hatch?" Irene asked.

"Yes, ma'am."

"Good," she said, delighted while keeping her gaze on the exodus. "Because I can definitely promise you this—you'll never forget this moment."

She gave Jamal a quick glance. "You see, young man, those turtles out there have a natural instinct, a strong drive to get into that water no matter how dangerous the journey. That's what you call perseverance. You know, we can learn something from nature if we took the time to be silent and just watch. Did you know that?"

Jamal shook his head. "No."

"Well, now you know," she said, standing. Irene walked to the water's edge to get a closer view.

I leaned into Jamal. "I know that was a little deep. But my sister *really* likes sea turtles."

Jamal and I spent the next several hours under the warm sun playing in shallow water, collecting seashells, building sand sculptures, and poking washed up dead jellyfish while Irene lounged underneath a big umbrella either sleeping or reading a book. Not once did she ever get into the water. Too scared of getting her tied-up hair wet, I guess.

Chapter 7

IT was almost six o'clock in the evening by the time we returned home from the beach. Jamal got out of the car and waited for Irene to unlock the trunk. "I'm sorry. I totally forgot to take you home," Irene said, smiling at Jamal.

"That's okay. I live just down the street. I can walk." He grabbed his bag. Then he turned to me and waved. "See you later."

"Hey wait," I called, stopping him. "What are you doing for the Fourth of July?"

He shrugged. "I'm not sure. I guess my mom will make some hot dogs and stuff or we'll just end up at one of her friend's house. What are you doing?"

"Well, we always have a cook out and then, at night, watch the town hall's fireworks light up the sky. Do you want to come over and eat with us?" I asked, nodding with an exaggerated grin. "There's going to be a lot of food. Plus, you can bring your mom and sister."

"A lot of food, huh?"

"Yep, like a buffet."

"Okay, I'll make sure to tell my mom about it," he said, stepping back.

"Wait! Don't take another step!" I ordered. I bent over and plucked a baby garden snake off the driveway. "You almost swashed it."

Jamal's eyes bugged out and then he took off.

"You're nasty, Lovely!" he yelled, running down the street.

"What!" I laughed. "It's just a harmless garden snake."

"Lovely!" Mama shouted from the porch. "Put that thing down and stop scaring that boy."

"Yes, ma'am." I released the snake in the grass.

"Did you enjoy yourself today?" she asked as I walked toward the porch.

"Yes ma'am."

"Good, now go to the side of the house and rinse your feet and legs off with the water hose before coming inside. I don't want you and Irene tracking sand on my clean floors."

I rinsed off and then entered the house through the laundry room. "Lovely, there's a towel on top of the washing machine. Make sure you dry off good," Mama hollered from the kitchen.

I walked behind Daddy sitting in his favorite reclining chair in the den. He was watching another episode of that new show *The Joy of Painting with Bob Ross*. I thought it was boring, but Daddy said it was soothing.

"Were there a lot this year?" he asked me as I headed toward the kitchen.

"Yes, sir—dozens."

Walking into the kitchen, I could see Mama had spent her day shopping and getting ready for the holiday on Wednesday because there were grocery bags everywhere. Aunt Harriet was over sitting at the table peeling and cutting up potatoes into a big plastic bowl while Mama tossed chicken around in a brown paper bag of flour.

"Mama, isn't it too early to start cooking for the Fourth of July?"

"Yes it is, honey, but it's never too early to get organized. You see, half of those potatoes are for tonight's dinner, and the other half will be used for the cookout. I'm making fried chicken and potato salad tonight."

From the corner of my eye, I caught Aunt Harriet giving me a strange look.

"What in the world is going on with your hair?" she asked bluntly. "Child, you look like Buckwheat's little sister."

Mama chuckled.

"Oh, stop it, Harriet. I told you the girls went to the beach this morning. She looks like she had fun."

"Well, I hope so with that big bush sitting on top of her head like that."

"Yeah, but you've got a point," Mama said, blowing out a long sigh. "Lovely sure has a lot of hair. Where will I find time to wash and press it for church in the morning?"

Mama dried her hands with an orange dishtowel and then walked over to pick through my hair. "Lovely, as soon as Irene is done in the bathroom, I want you to take a shower and wash your hair just like I showed you, all right. That should save me some time."

"Yes ma'am," I said, turning to leave.

"And, oh, did you get a chance to invite Jamal and his family to the cookout?" she asked.

I stopped. "Yes, ma'am, I did."

"Good," Mama said. "I hope they come, because I would love to finally meet Jamal's mother."

I gave Mama a quick smile and then kept on walking toward my bedroom. In the background, I heard Aunt Harriet ask, "Dolores, didn't you invite that woman and her children to church?"

"Yes, I did."

"Well, I still haven't seen them there. But I guarantee they'll show up for some free food."

I shook my head and rolled my eyes listening to that. If the Turners did decide to come over, I just hope Aunt Harriet would be nice and not embarrass me by badgering Mrs. Turner about church.

Chapter 8

"YES! Give another round of applause for the choir's final selection: 'To God Be the Glory,' led by the very talented Anika Douglas," said Pastor Holmes. The congregation continued to clap until the organist signaled the benediction.

Pastor Holmes stretched his arms out. "As we disperse praising God and giving Him the glory, I ask the Lord to bless each and every one of you and let his light be your guide—Amen."

"Amen!" the crowd repeated.

"Also, one last announcement," the pastor continued. As most of you already know, there's been a lot of talk among the community about the Highway 50 extension project. For those who are interested in hearing more about the proposal or would just like to voice their concerns or opinions, please remain behind to get a flyer for the time and date of the town hall meeting."

Anika and I waved at each other, not paying attention to grown-up talk. She was taking off her white and gold choir rob and putting it on a hanger. Today, her plaits, pinned up into a French roll, were sort of plain—something like mine. There were no colorful beads or wild design pattern decorating her head.

Anika walked up to me smiling. "I like your cornrows," she said, examining my two jumbo pigtails. "This is the first time I've ever seen your hair braided."

"Thanks." I touched my head. "Mama was really tired yesterday and didn't feel like messing with my hair."

"Well, you know I like it. You should wear it like this more often."

I returned the compliment with a wide smile.

"So, are you coming to my cookout this year?" I asked.

"I can't." She frowned. "We're going to my cousin's house in Mt. Pleasant...sorry."

"Uh, that's okay. I just wanted you to meet Jamal."

"Oh, yes, your boyfriend." She fluttered her eyelashes.

"Stop it, Anika. You know darn well he's just a good friend."

"Whatever you say, Lovely." A puzzled look came across Anika's face. "Why don't you just invite Jamal to church? That way I can definitely meet him."

Not this question again!

"I've already done that. And I'm not sure he'll ever come."

"That's not surprising," Anika said. "Most boys don't like going to church anyway. You rarely see my dad here, right?"

"I'm telling you, Joseph, I don't like the sound of it," I heard Mama say behind me. "I don't care how much money this extension is going to bring to our town." I turned my head because she sounded upset and saw her walking up the aisle with a flyer in hand.

She stopped in front of us.

"Hello Anika. How are you doing this morning?" she asked.

"I'm fine, ma'am."

"Good." She nodded, looking quite serious. "I enjoyed your performance today, baby. So keep up the good work."

"Thank you, Mrs. Duval. I will."

"Lovely, it's time to go. Tell Anika goodbye."

I turned to Anika wide-eyed. "I guess I'll see you next week."

It was obvious Anika noticed Mama's unusual mood and responded simply with a head nod and wave. I didn't completely understand what the town of Willisburg was doing to get underneath Mama's skin, but the entire trip home she kept saying it was wrong.

Chapter 9

WE got up early to get the yard situated just the way Mama wanted for the cookout. Mama assigned me and Irene to light duties but hired the neighbor's thirty-three-year-old son, Alvin, to do the hard work—mowing the lawn, trimming the hedges, and setting up two heavy foldout tables under the Elm tree—while she followed behind and draped red and white checkered table clothes over them.

Mama called Alvin special. That was her polite way of not calling him slow or retarded like some people did around here. She said just because he talked funny and had a learning disability, it didn't make him stupid.

"I don't care what folks say about that boy. He may not have book smarts, but he sure does beautiful yard work and takes pride in it," Mama said two summers ago. As far as she was concerned, Alvin had always been a nice, respectful young man ever since he was a child. And for fifteen dollars and the promise of all he could eat at the cookout, it didn't take much to convince him to help out this morning. He was happy to do it. As a matter of fact, that man never stopped grinning even in the high noon heat.

I was beginning to think I was taking my job as decorator a little too far when I looked down and realized the large bag of mini US flags was almost empty—all one hundred of them.

I looked around. I was supposed to only outline the flower beds in front of the porch and put a few of them in a candy bowl for the other kids, but I ended up outlining one side of the entire driveway with mini flags.

"Lovely, what are you doing, child? Pull some of those out of the ground. You've got this yard looking like Arlington Cemetery," Mama said from underneath her wide brim sun hat.

Irene laughed while sweeping the porch. "That's right, Lovely, we're not expecting the president of the United States to stop by."

I flashed Irene a silly smirk before bending over to uproot my handiwork. I guess I was feeling creative, just like the time I put a gazillion stickers on my bicycle.

"Telephone, Lovely!" Daddy hollered from the front door.

"Who is it, Joseph? Don't you see she's helping me in yard?" Mama said.

"I forgot his name. It's that boy from down the street."

I turned to Mama. "Can I?"

Mama sighed. "Make it fast, young lady. We still got work to do."

"Yes, ma'am," I said, running to the phone.

I raised the yellow receiver to my ear. "Hello."

"Hi Lovely," Jamal said cheerfully.

"Hi! Are you coming to my cookout?"

"Yeah, that's the plan. But my cousin's here. Can he come too?"

"I don't see why not. But, hold on. Let me ask my mom."

I opened the front door and stuck my head out. "Mama, can Jamal bring his cousin to the cookout?"

"Sure, we've got plenty," she said, unfolding tan metal chairs on the porch. I ran back to the phone excited.

"She said yes, Jamal."

"Okay, great. What time should we come over?"

"Mama said the food should be done around three o'clock. So, how old is your cousin?"

"Oh, he's twelve and a half."

"Lovely, I need you to come back out here and help your Aunt Harriet," Mama hollered.

"Jamal, I've got to go. See you later."

I hung up the phone and then ran outside. Looking straight ahead into the distance, I saw Aunt Harriet waiting to cross the road with a bunch of plastic bags in her hands.

A white pickup truck zoomed by.

"And they wanna extend that road," I heard Mama grumble as I went down the steps.

"Stop right there, Lovely," Mama shouted just as I reached the edge of the yard. "Let Harriet come to you."

I looked back. "Yes, ma'am," I said, wondering what all the fuss was about. Any other time, Mama wouldn't think twice about trusting me to cross the street to pick up or drop off something by myself.

Aunt Harriet lifted her arms and kinda hobbled into the grass.

Where's Cynthia? I wondered.

"Why isn't Cynthia helping you?" I asked while unloading one of her hands.

She was winded. "Child, I wasn't going to wait for her. That girl's still in the bathroom fixing her hair. She's at that age, you know."

My lips curled up in confusion. *Who's Cynthia primping for? There aren't any boys her age coming to the cookout.*

"I hear you huffin' and puffin' for air out there, girl," Mama yelled jokingly across the yard. "You're four years younger than me, and I swear I'm in better shape than you are."

"Oh hush up," she said, approaching the porch. The second Aunt Harriet reached the bottom of the steps, she dropped the bags then started bobbing her head.

"The yard looks good, Dolores," she said, taking in a deep breath, both hands holding her plump hips. "The hedges and hanging plants are nice. I even like the decorations."

"Thank you!" I spoke up, feeling like I deserved the praise.

"Yes, thank you." Mama snickered then took a glance at me. "But you know Alvin did most of the work?"

"I'm sure he did. That boy is definitely good with his hands."

Aunt Harriet turned her head and shouted to Alvin who was bent over tossing red mulch around a small tree. He stood up and walked over.

"Yes, ma'am," he said, still wearing that big grin.

"Alvin, I want you to do some landscaping in my yard next weekend. Can you do that for me? I'll pay ya good."

"Oh, yes, ma'am." He nodded.

Mama took off her hat and then started fanning herself with it. "Well, I think I've done all I can out here. I best get cleaned up and get the food going. It's already eleven and three o'clock will be here before you know it."

Mama stuck her hand into her pocket and pulled out some money. "Here, Alvin." She stretched her arm out with a smile. "Thank you for your help, hun. Now, go on home and get washed up so you can come back and eat with us."

"Yeah…and put on something nice like one of those Clemson T-shirts you like to wear. You've always looked good in orange," Irene said.

I didn't think it was possible, but Alvin's smile got even wider. This time his grin was so big, I could count almost all of his teeth.

"Okay, Irene, I'll wear it just for you," he said excitedly then walked away.

"There you go, Irene," Aunt Harriet said as she picked up the bags and headed toward the front door.

"There I go—what?" Irene asked.

"You know—making that boy fall in love with you, again," Aunt Harriet replied.

"Again!" I blurted then stuck my tongue out in disgust thinking about the two of them kissing.

"That's right, Lovely," Aunt Harriet laughed. "Alvin used to have a big ole crush on Irene back in the day when they were kids. That boy would do anything to get Irene's attention. He'd pick her flowers and carry her schoolbooks. Remember, Irene?"

Irene groaned. "Please...don't remind me."

"Well, I still think he likes her," Mama jumped in.

"Oh, no ma'am!" Irene responded, wide-eyed. "Let's keep the past—in the past."

Aunt Harriet opened the screen door. "I don't know, Irene, you may want to reconsider that, especially, since you're thirty-four years old and still single with no children. Time's a wasting."

Irene gave Aunt Harriet an obvious fake smile. "You don't have to concern yourself with my love life, Auntie. I'm doing just fine."

After Aunt Harriet walked into the house, Irene rolled her eyes then looked back at me. I couldn't help but give her a gloating grin. She teased me so hard about Jamal the other day. Now it was her turn to get a dose of her own medicine.

Chapter 10

THE cookout didn't get jumping until a little after 4:00. Mama said people were coming in late because of the heat. Aunt Harriet said black folk never arrive or start events on time. With the temperature being around eighty-two degrees and Aunt Harriet taking an hour just to buy a bag of charcoal from the corner store, I thought it was a little bit of both.

We had a huge turnout. More than I expected. There were cars parked almost bumper-to-bumper in the driveway and on the side of the street. And those who couldn't find a space near our yard ended up parking in the open field across the street next to Aunt Harriet's house.

I recognized most folks, but some I had no clue who they were. It was like Mama went uptown and handed out flyers at the Piggly Wiggly asking the whole town to come out. Thank goodness a lot of them came with either drinks or dishes of their own. Mama called it a potluck. I called it sharing the load. But even though it seemed like the entire neighborhood was here, Jamal was nowhere in sight.

"Put one of those burnt hotdogs on a bun for me," Aunt Harriet shouted from the table to Addie who was guarding the grill like a food cop. Addie said there were too many greedy people and curious little hands reaching for the grill. And if she hadn't taken charge, the bar-b-que would have gone an hour ago.

Whodini's "Friends" was playing loudly in the background.

Some older teenager I'd seen at church before ran a long orange extension cord from the living room window through the yard to set up turn-tables and speakers. Now group of kids were standing in front of him, dancing, while he spun records.

"What is that?" Mama asked.

"Oh, that's a new of type music the young folk are listening to these days," Ms. Lorraine answered. "My grandson told me it's called rap. If you ask me, it's a bunch of noise. "

"No, I'm not talking about the music, Lorraine. I'm talking about that dance move."

The kids were jerking their arms and heads back and forth to the beat of the song.

"Oh, that's the *whop*," I said, jumping in the conversation. "I saw it on *Soul Train*."

"Well, why aren't you out there, Lovely?" Mama asked. "Let me see you do it."

"Yeah, go have some fun with Deidra and Cynthia and those other children," Aunt Harriet added.

I liked the music and saw everyone having fun, but I just didn't feel like going out there. Maybe I didn't want to dance in front of strangers. Maybe I was still looking for Jamal.

"Oh, I'll go later," I said.

"Do you see Deidra out there shaking her behind? She just turned thirteen, right, Dolores?" Aunt Harriet asked.

I rolled my eyes then took a glance at Mama to get her reaction. Her eyes were narrowed and focused. Something in the distance caught her attention. But I didn't know what.

"Yes," Mama answered, never taking her gaze off whatever was distracting her.

Then suddenly Mama hollered, "Get out of the road, child!"

That's when I finally saw what Mama was seeing. A little boy, about six, was chasing after a kick-ball that had rolled into the street. But Mama's loud voice alerted a nearby woman who grabbed the boy just as two cars were coming down the road.

"Now, that's a good reason why I am so dead set against expanding that road," Mama griped. "It's already too dangerous."

"What are you talking about, Dolores? Those cars weren't speeding. I think you're worrying about that expansion project more than you should. All they want to do is connect our highway to Interstate 95 so we can attract a little more business in town. I really don't see how that's gonna make this area dangerous."

"Well, if not dangerous, then too noisy," Mama snapped. "This has always been a quiet, small community. Isn't that why you and Richard decided to buy that house across the street in the first place?"

"Yes, it is," Aunt Harriet agreed. "But we're just a speck of dirt on a large map. Who's coming here? And—"

"Now, Dolores, you know these are just the signs of the time," Ms. Lorraine interrupted. "Take a look around. Everything is changing: music, clothes—we've got boys wearing tight leather pants and eyeliner, for heaven's sake. And don't get me started on those computers—everything's speeding up. It was just a matter of time until our township would want to keep up with everyone else. But, I bet you'll have your say at the town hall meeting this Thursday. Won't you? "

"You've got that right, Lorraine, because I still think it's a bad idea."

Mama shook her head as she switched her sight toward the crowd. "Look at them," she continued. "Irene and those kids are still dancing. Where do they find the energy? You know they say *youth* is wasted on the young... Well, I'm beginning to agree. They have the youth. But they lack the wisdom—just like those younger folks who run this town and wanna change up everything."

"Now, look at that!" Aunt Harriet said, sounding surprised.

"What?" Mama asked.

My face shifted. It was Jamal and his family walking across the lawn.

I took a glimpse at my Mickey Mouse watch; it was 5:27 PM. *Better late than never*, I said to myself. The moment my eyes met Jamal's, I smiled. Then he waved. His clothes were neat and coordinated, as usual, and so were his mother's and little sister's. Mrs. Turner was carrying a pan covered with foil wrap. She must've gotten the memo about the potluck.

The taller boy walking next to Jamal had to be his cousin. I didn't see anything special about him, but Deidra and some other girls sure did, because they started giggling when he passed by. Maybe they liked his Jheri curl and the red and white striped sweatband around his head. To me he looked like a wannabe break-dancer.

Mama stood up and extended her hands when Mrs. Turner arrived at the table.

"Thank you, Gwen, and it's nice to finally meet you," Mama said warmly, taking the pan.

"Oh, you're welcome, Mrs. Duval. Those are just some baked beans I whipped up. And, yes, it's nice to meet you too."

"Well, you can just call me Dolores," Mama said, then started to point. "This is my sister Harriet, and this is my friend, Lorraine."

Aunt Harriet and Ms. Lorraine nodded with polite smiles then said their hellos. But I kept my eyes on Aunt Harriet, praying silently she'd be on her best behavior and not say anything rude.

"Hello, nice to meet you all," Mrs. Turner replied.

"Well, I think most of us know Jamal's face around here; he and Lovely have become good friends over the summer. But we don't know who these two young people are."

"Oh, yes. This is my daughter, Nicole, and my nephew, Terrence."

Mama nodded with a smile and then turned to me.

"Lovely, why don't you take this pan and put in the oven so it can warm up."

I sprang up. "Yes, ma'am."

I looked at Jamal and signaled him to follow me.

"I thought you weren't coming," I said as we walked inside the house.

"Yeah, sorry about being late. But we had company and my mom didn't want to come over until it got cooler."

"That's okay. I was just bored not having someone to talk to."

I opened the warm oven and slid the pan next to a large tray stacked with grilled hamburgers, hot dog wieners, and ribs. I sniffed then turned around.

"Are you hungry?"

After loading our plates, we sat down on the front porch steps to eat. People were still buzzing about—enjoying the music and food while fireworks popped near and far as the sun started to set.

"You know, the colorful fireworks are best seen from the field. Do you want to go over there later tonight?" I asked, biting into a slice of watermelon.

"Sure," he answered, and then chomped into a monster burger built with two patties, cheese, and a wiener on top with ketchup and mustard oozing from the sides.

I stared in amazement. "Where do you put it all?"

"What? I'm hungry."

Suddenly, the music turned up. "Party people...get on the dance floor!" the DJ shouted.

"Can you dance, Jamal?"

"Nope," he said without taking his eyes off his sandwich.

"Go 'head, go 'head, go 'head, go 'head..." people in the yard cheered.

Apparently, Terrence had taken center stage by bustin' some moves. And sure enough, Deidra was already in his face acting like a silly groupie.

"Hey, is your cousin really a break-dancer?"

Jamal rolled his eyes and sucked his teeth. "Were you really delivered by a stork in the middle of the night?"

I nodded my head. "Gotcha."

Chapter 11

LOUD explosions and bursts of bright colors filled the night sky. And just as promised, we had the best view sitting on a blanket in the open field. Our spot was perfect. It felt as though Jamal and I were the only two out there underneath the stars, but we weren't alone. There were other people scattered around standing, sitting on lawn chairs, or on the hoods of cars enjoying the show. It was like watching the Fourth of July celebration on a giant outdoor movie screen.

For me, this wasn't anything new. Growing up here, I'd seen this light show plenty times before. But it was another first for Jamal. Even in the darkness, I could see his excited eyes behind those glasses. And the way he tilted his head back to follow shooting fireworks told me he was really impressed.

"I told you you'd like it." I grinned while unfolding a napkin stacked with chocolate chip cookies. I reached out and offered half.

"Thanks," he said, throwing one into his mouth. "And you're right—this is the best way to watch fireworks."

"Well, my mama said that's the benefit of living in the country. There are no city lights or tall buildings around here to block our view. All we have are porch lights and the stars above our heads to light our way."

"Your family members sure have a lot of sayings." He chuckled.

I chuckled inside knowing he was right. "They sure do."

"Well, the only thing my mama ever says is, 'You better not lie to me boy, because if you lie...you'll steal.'"

A tiny smile appeared on Jamal's face and then he shrugged his shoulders. I smiled back, but what he said made me think of his dad. I didn't want to be nosy, but I couldn't help it.

"Jamal, can I ask you a question?"

"Yeah, go ahead."

"Did your father really go to jail for stealing?" I asked cautiously.

Jamal stared at me. His face paled. "How'd you know about that?"

"Like I've told you before, gossip spreads fast around here—doesn't matter if it's true or not."

Jamal looked straight ahead. "Yes and no," he answered.

My eyes shrunk into a confused squint. "What do you mean—yes and no?"

He sighed.

"Well, first, my mother's boyfriend *did* go to jail for robbing a convenient store, but he also shot a cop in the arm trying to get away. And, secondly, that guy's not my father. He's Nicole's dad." Jamal shrugged again like it didn't matter. "I actually don't know who my father is. Mama just said he wanted to be free."

"So, your mom isn't married then?"

"Nope." He shook his head. "Never has been."

Jamal seemed sad. He didn't even touch his last cookie.

"Well, that's something else we have in common."

"Yeah, what's that?"

"I don't know who my real father is either. So you're not alone."

A sudden explosion of green sparkles filled the entire sky, turning our clothes and everything around us into emerald green. It was the finale. We turned to each other with cheerful grins.

"Ooh, that was a good one!" And right after I said that, I heard what sounded like giggles coming from Aunt Harriet's house.

"Did you hear that?" I looked around Jamal's head.

"Hear what?" He turned.

The giggling started up again.

"That!" I whispered.

He glanced at me. "Yeah, I did that time."

I picked up my flashlight and led the way to investigate. We ended up at the back of the house, creeping and acting like detectives with toothy grins.

"Be quiet," I whispered, wide-eyed. "They're on the other side of house. When I count to three, we're going to run and catch them, okay?"

Jamal nodded excitedly.

"One, two, three—let's go!"

We made a dash to bum-rush whoever was around the corner. And that's how we caught them—Deidra pressed up against the side of the house with Terrence's hand down her pants.

"Ooh, Imma tell Addie you out here doing the nasty," I said, aiming my flashlight.

"Lovely, get that damn light out of my face," Deidra hissed in a low voice. She snatched the flashlight out of my hand, turned it off, and then threw it into the dark woods. Only the dim, yellow light bulb on the back porch gave us light to see.

"You didn't have to do that, Deidra!" I yelled.

"Shut up!" she whispered through clenched teeth, trying hard not to get busted. "If you weren't acting like a little baby by spying on me, I wouldn't of thrown your stupid flashlight into the woods."

"I'm not a baby," I said, giving her the evil eye. "And who's going to get my flashlight?"

"Oh, yeah—well, if you ain't no baby, then go into those woods and get it yourself."

"You threw it!" I snapped. "Why should I have to go in there? Deidra, if you don't get my flashlight then I'm really going to tell Addie."

"Well, go ahead and tell her—I'll just lie." She smirked.

"Hey, hey, hold up. Nobody needs to tell anyone anything. I know how we can fix this," Terrence butted in. "Lovely, you said you're not a baby, right?"

"That's right."

"So, check this out. If you kiss Jamal, I'll get your flashlight for you."

"What!" I said, making a grossed-out face.

Kiss a boy? No way!

"C'mon, Lovely, it shouldn't be so hard. Don't you like my cousin?"

"Yeah, but as a friend."

"Well, just give my man a quick, friendly kiss on the lips."

I turned to Jamal. He looked just as uncomfortable as I was.

"You don't have to do anything, Lovely," Jamal said. "We can just come back tomorrow and search for it during the daytime."

"Yeah, but you said you weren't a baby," Terrence teased.

"Oh, grow up, Lovely. You're going to be in middle school soon. This is what middle-schoolers do. Don't be such a big baby!"

I didn't like being teased and I definitely wasn't chicken. I thought about what was worse—kissing Jamal or letting my favorite, red flashlight that was decorated with glitter get dirty or damaged in the woods overnight. *I don't think so!*

"I'm not a baby!" I declared then walked over to Jamal and kissed him dead on the lips.

"Problem solved," Terrence proclaimed. "Now you both have something on each other. Plus, my little cuz just got his first kiss. Bam…I'm good!"

Terrence pulled a lighter out of his pocket then headed for the woods. Deidra followed behind cackling. "You so smart, Terrence," I heard her say.

"Yeah, she's not going to tell on you," he said, sounding proud of himself. "Telling on you would be like telling on herself."

I rolled my eyes then looked at Jamal. "No one calls me a baby!"

Chapter 12

IF *I had a time machine, I'd go back to Wednesday night and stop myself from kissing Jamal.* That was the only wish looping in my head as I stood in front of my white dresser and mirror and performed my nightly routine of rubbing moisturizer into my hair and then combing it through.

It had been three days since the incident with Deidra and three days since I'd spoken to Jamal. When I called him on Thursday, Ms. Turner said he wasn't available. But she'd have him call me back. I never got that call. I'd been thinking maybe Jamal was mad at me for kissing him.

I heard Mama's voice at the front door. She didn't sound too happy. I cracked my bedroom door to listen in.

"I don't know why they even bother to have a town hall meeting," Mama said to Irene. "If you ask me, the whole 'We want to hear your concerns' was just a show, because it took them less than ten minutes to come to unanimous vote to approve that project."

"I know, Mama. But the residents of this town made it so easy for them to do what they wanted. No one really showed up to protest. Well, at least you got the chance to speak your mind and get your objection on record."

"Yeah, I guess you're right, Irene. At least I can say I tried."

I heard tapping behind me.

I turned. The noise was coming from my window.

Tap. Tap, I heard again, then my name in a whisper.

"Who is that?" I murmured, pulling back the curtain.

It was Jamal peering at me. I lifted the window.

"What are you doing here? Do you know what time it is? It's almost nine o'clock at night."

Jamal chuckled. "I know. Can I come in?"

"Are you crazy?" I replied. "My mama will let me have it if she catches you in here."

"Lovely."

The sound of Mama's soft voice made me jump.

"Yes, ma'am," I answered, moving quickly to the door." I opened it.

"I just wanted to let you know that I'm home. Are you all right?"

"Yes, ma'am." I nodded.

"Good. Sleep tight. I'll talk to you in the morning." Mama leaned over and kissed my forehead. I shut the door, locked it, and then ran back to the window where Jamal was still waiting.

I pushed the window open wider. "Okay, I'll let you in. But only for a few minutes," I whispered, helping him in. "So what's so important it couldn't wait until tomorrow?"

Jamal let out a big sigh. He looked serious.

"Oh, I just needed to get out of the house. My mom's boyfriend is over and they're arguing."

Arguing—I don't think I've ever heard my parents really argue. I felt bad for him.

"I'm sorry, Jamal. Are you all right?"

"Yeah, I'm okay. I just don't want to hear them right now."

I nodded then walked over to the dresser to pick up my comb before sitting on the bed.

"Do they always fight?"

"No," he said. "But it won't be long until it becomes an everyday thing. It usually does. You know, I don't want my mom to be alone, but she seems to be a magnet for losers. The good thing is, I'm sure she's gonna dump him."

"How do you know that?"

"I know because most of her relationships don't last. I like to use the year test. If she dates a guy for a year, then it's serious. "

Jamal took the comb out of my hand. I turned around and gave him a curious stare.

"What are you doing?"

He sucked his teeth. "Oh, turn back around and chill out. I do Nicole's hair all the time."

Jamal parted my hair down the middle and then began braiding. Sitting there, I wanted to ask him why he never returned my phone call and was he angry with me for kissing him? But I decided to skip those questions altogether and forget the kiss ever happened. I just figured he couldn't be that upset, because he wouldn't be here fixing my hair.

"You have nice hair," he said.

"Thanks, I've been told I inherited it from my birth mom."

"Lovely?"

"Yeah?"

"I know you were adopted. But, seriously, you've never met your mother before?"

I looked at him. "That's correct. I've never met my birth mom or dad before. I know my mom's name is Corinne Scott. And she and Irene were friends. I mean, I've seen an old picture of her from Irene's college yearbook, but that's it. And I know absolutely nothing about my birth father."

"The same goes for Cynthia too, right?"

"Yep."

"Well, do you and Cynthia ever talk about her? And has anyone ever told you why your mother gave you two up?"

"No. Not really. Cynthia doesn't like talking about her. I can tell by the facial expressions she makes whenever I try to bring her up. And as for why Corinne gave us up for adoption, I'm not sure." I shook my head. "Irene and Mama just told us having babies wasn't in our mother's plans. And by the tone of their voices, I don't think they like talking about her either."

"Wow, that's some heavy stuff," Jamal said. "It sounds almost unbelievable."

"Well, trust me, it's all true. I'm living proof of it."

"Lovely?"

"Yeah."

"Do you hate her?" Jamal asked, working on the last braid.

I got quiet for a minute. His question made me think hard. I wasn't sure how I felt about my birth mother. "I don't know," I finally answered. "I never think about her long enough to feel anything."

Jamal tapped me on the shoulder. "Hey, I'm done. Go take a look."

I got up and looked in the mirror. Jamal braided my hair into two neat cornrows. "Not bad, Jamal," I said, pleased. "I'm coming back to you again when Mama's too tired to fix my hair."

He smirked. "I told you I knew what I was doing."

I turned around and gave him a quick hug. "Jamal, I'm glad you're here. And I'm glad you're my friend."

Chapter 13

THE school year started without a hitch. Luckily, Jamal and I landed in the same homeroom. And, as expected, we were like two peas in a pod sitting next to each other on the bus and in some classes. But as time went on, we managed to make a few friends of our own. After being in school for one month, I started eating lunch with Sabrina Thompson, a girl I met in home economics class.

It was the end of October. I had just turned eleven, and the C.C. Johnson Middle School sixth grade dance was only a week away. That's all everyone talked about—what people were going to wear and who was going with who. I didn't care about the dance at all, but Mama said it was a good opportunity to be social and meet more people. Sabrina basically laid on a guilt trip by telling me she wouldn't go to the dance unless I went—but she *really* wanted to go—so I should go.

But I wasn't the only one on the hook to attend this silly dance.

Jamal got bullied into going with Victoria Stevens, a bossy sixth grader who asked me if I was dating Jamal a few weeks ago. Naturally, I told her no. So, she immediately told Jamal they were going to the dance together because she knew he didn't have a girlfriend or a date for the dance. Jamal said I should have lied. "I didn't know she was going to ask you to the dance," I told him.

***

A week went by faster than a cookie in Jamal's hand. I spent all of Saturday morning getting ready for that night's dance. And, of course, most of that time was spent on getting my hair pressed, curled, and then pinned up into a side ponytail—a hairstyle Sabrina showed me from *Teen Magazine* and who, with bugged-out eyes, told me I should get it done. But that was *so* Sabrina to stay on top of the latest fashion and music trends. She often got excited about anything dealing with teenage stuff, even though we were only eleven years old. Obviously, the teen bug hadn't bitten me yet, but hanging out with Sabrina kept me in the loop of things and made me feel less of an outsider.

I sat at one of several round tables in the gym decorated with purple and gold top hats and string confetti—clashing with our school colors in my yellow and fuchsia party dress. Before leaving the house, Mama took Polaroid pictures of my hair for memory's sake. She said it looked pretty. But I shouldn't expect such a fancy hairstyle every weekend because it was too much work.

Sabrina was sitting next to me yapping with some other girl about a group of boys at a nearby table. While they gossiped, I sat wondering why I was there when I could be home in my bedroom reading a book or figuring out what in the world this weird sensation was I had in my stomach all day. That's when Victoria walked in with Jamal. I could see her gigantic smile from across the room.

"Wow!" I murmured. Not only did Victoria pick him up, she even made Jamal wear a black dress shirt to match her green and black striped dress.

"Talk about being a Bossy Mc-Nossy," I murmured again.

I caught Jamal's attention with a wave. He flashed one of his fake smiles I'd seen plenty times before and then waved back. He didn't look happy. But that wasn't my fault. If he didn't want to come to the dance with Victoria Stevens, he should have told her no. And Mama agreed. That was another thing I'd been wondering today. Was Jamal's reluctance to claim Victoria just a show because he really liked her?

"Is that Jamal with Victoria?" Sabrina asked. "He actually looks kinda cute."

"Yeah, I guess so."

"Are you jealous?" She grinned.

"Why should I be? We're just friends."

Sabrina gasped. "Oh...my...gosh!" she shrieked then leaned into my ear. "Don't look now, but you won't believe who's staring at you."

"Who?" I asked, holding still but trying hard to see from the corners of my eyes.

"It's Sean Patterson. He is *soo* fine," she squealed. "He's to the right of you. Just act natural and turn slowly."

I had no idea who Sean Patterson was. So I discreetly turned my head, as instructed, not knowing what to expect. But Sabrina was right. He was cute and still looking straight at me. Sean gave me a smile and a wave. I froze for a second, but then mustered up enough courage to do the same.

Prince's "Baby I'm a Star" started playing.

"I love this song!" Sabrina shouted, running her fingers through her freshly cropped mushroom hairstyle she said was inspired by Tootie from the show the *Facts of Life*.

"I'm going to go dance. Are you coming, Lovely?"

Sabrina shot up out of her seat and started dancing toward a bunch of girls on the dance floor. She looked back at me and shouted, "Come on, Lovely. Come on!"

An enthusiastic smile grew on my face. "Okay," I shouted back. After all, I did like the song too.

I started dancing. It was so much fun jumping and twirling around. I couldn't stop grinning. Then I felt a tap on my shoulder. It was Sean dancing next to me. Sabrina gave me a wide-eyed stare. "Oh my gosh!" she mouthed as she waved goodbye and danced away.

"Hi, I'm Sean," he shouted over the loud music.

"I'm Lovely," I yelled back.

The song ended and a slow one started up. Sean and I just stood there, giving each other awkward glances. Then suddenly, he stretched out his arms.

"May I?" he asked.

Instantly, I froze, not knowing what to do. I had never slow danced before. I turned to look for Sabrina. She was already tethered to a boy. When our eyes met, she bobbed her head, giving me encouragement to dance with him.

"Yes," I answered, feeling nervous.

Sean placed his hands on my waist and I put hands on his shoulders like I'd seen on TV. Then, slowly, we turned around in circles. I couldn't believe I was slow dancing.

And that's when it happened. Something strange was going on between my legs. I felt wetness on my underwear—like I had peed a little. I stopped and pulled away from Sean.

"Is everything okay?" he asked.

"I'm not sure," I replied, feeling confused. "Ah, I've gotta go. Thanks for the dance."

As I walked off fast, I caught a glimpse of Jamal watching me while he danced with Victoria. He looked concerned. I got Sabrina's attention and signaled her to follow me into the bathroom. When I got into the bathroom stall, I quickly pulled down my panties and to my surprise…there was blood.

I cringed. "Oh my God!"

"What? What's wrong?" Sabrina asked, from the other side of the door.

"Sabrina, I need you to call my sister. I think I just got my period. "

Chapter 14

IRENE hummed sweetly while washing my back—just like she used to when combing my hair before I started doing it on my own. The water was warm with extra bubbles and smelled like lavender. Irene said it was a special time for me now that I had my period. And, as a young lady, having good personal hygiene would be the most important thing from here on out.

Before getting in the tub, she showed me how to put on a sanitary napkin and then how to wrap it up and dispose of it properly. "Make sure you change these pads throughout the day as they fill up. Trust me...you do not want to be walking around smelling like dead, old fish," she warned.

To me, all of it seemed to be happening really fast—the added responsibility of keeping up with my periods, worrying about blood leaking through my clothes during school, and smelling like stinky old trout was too much. *Why now? Sex education class doesn't even start until next semester.*

"Why has my period come so early?" I whined.

Irene chuckled. "Oh, girl, please. My menstrual cycle started early too. And it came right in front of everyone in gym class."

"In front of everyone!" I exclaimed.

"Yes, Lovely. I had a big red spot on the back of my white shorts."

I turned around. "Yeah, but I'm the only one out of my friends who has a period. And worse—it started while dancing with Sean Patterson. "

"Lovely," Irene said with a warm smile, "you're not the first girl to go through this phase of life. I went through this, Mama went through this, and soon enough, all of your girlfriends will go through the same thing too. So don't worry. This is just puberty—nature's way of slowly turning you into a woman and preparing your body for motherhood. And as for that boy, Sean, he wouldn't be alive on this earth today if it weren't for his mother's periods."

I turned my back to Irene and she began washing it again. Then I thought about motherhood. Listening to Irene's advice made me wonder why she'd never gotten married or had any kids of her own. I always thought she'd be a good mother. She was already a wonderful big sister and definitely pretty. There were so many times I'd watch her get dressed up for something and wished I had her curly, soft hair and light brown eyes.

When it came to looks, Irene took more after Daddy—and that included his high yellow skin, as Aunt Harriet would jokingly call it. The story goes…daddy's great grandfather was a white Frenchman who settled in New Orleans and fell in love with a black Creole woman. They had a bunch of children, but unfortunately, there were no known photographs of them or the couple. Somehow, over time, the Duval family got scattered to the wind.

"Irene, do you think you'll ever have children someday?"

"Hmm, I'm not sure, Lovely. That's up to the good Lord. If He wants me to have a family, I guess He'll put the right man in my path. But, for now, I'm happy with teaching my kids and watching over you—little girl." She gently poked my back, making me giggle.

"You know, Lovely, you may not call me Mama, but I certainly feel I've played a major part in your upbringing—watching you grow up in this house from a baby to the young lady you are now. Yep, in many ways, you're just like a daughter to me."

Hearing those words made me feel loved. I almost wanted to cry.

"Irene?"

"Yes, darling."

"I love you."

"Oh, I know. I love you too," she said, handing me the washcloth and then standing. "Listen kiddo, I've got to fill out an application for school. Do you think you can finish up here?"

I looked up and nodded with confidence.

"That's my girl." She winked. "But don't forget to do what I told you—wash your lady parts good."

Chapter 15

"SO, what's it like? Do you feel any different? I still can't believe you got your period before me," Sabrina whispered in class on Monday morning. I knew the moment I saw her walking down the aisle with that silly grin she'd have a million questions to ask—much more than Anika did in church yesterday.

"What do you mean?" I chuckled nervously, hoping no one around us could hear. "I feel the same."

"Well, when my sister got her period, she complained about having painful cramps. She even had to put a bottle of hot water on her stomach just to get some sleep. But, months later, she said it was all worth it because her boobs got bigger."

Sabrina grabbed my arm and squeezed it a little. "Ooh, I can't wait to get my period, Lovely! I can't wait until I develop boobs of my own."

The look on Sabrina's face was way too intense—like she was about to burst into pieces if she didn't start bleeding or sprout boobs that very instant. If you ask me, boobs were nothing but trouble. Last weekend Irene promised to take me shopping for a training bra. I didn't experience cramps like Sabrina's sister, but my tiny breasts were a little sore. I thought about sharing the news, but didn't dare. It would have crushed

Sabrina. I actually imagined her eyes popping out of their sockets along with steam shooting from her ears in frustration and jealousy.

***

When the school bus stopped, I made sure to get off fast. I had been avoiding a long conversation with Jamal all day. Even though he was a close friend, I was still too embarrassed to tell a *boy* about me getting my period. "Hey, wait up!" I heard him shout behind me. But I ignored him and kept on walking fast. "Lovely, stop. I'm trying to talk to you," he shouted again.

I stopped and turned around. "What? What do you want?"

"Well, you didn't return my phone call yesterday and you barely said a word to me today. So, what's up? Are you mad at me or something?" he asked.

He sounded concerned. I looked away and debated in my head if I should tell him or not.

"It's not you," I answered, still gazing off.

"Okay, then, what is it?"

"I don't know, Jamal. It's too embarrassing."

"Oh, c'mon! You can tell me; we're friends...remember?"

I took a deep breath and then looked straight into Jamal's eyes. "I got my period while dancing with Sean Patterson, okay?"

"So that's why you stormed off the dance floor."

"Yep." I nodded. "I'm just really glad nothing got on my dress."

"So what's the problem? I know what a period is," he said, shrugging.

"You do?" I was actually surprised.

"Yeah, that's when you bleed, right? My mom gets her period every month. And sometimes—she even has to soak her drawers in the bathroom sink just to get the blood out."

"Aww, that's disgusting, Jamal!"

"How's that disgusting?" He laughed. I was told a period was a gift from Mother Nature. And soon…you'll be soaking your gift in a sink too."

"Oh, shut up, you silly fool," I said, giving him a gentle shove.

We started walking again. And even though Jamal's ability to make everything a joke would usually annoy me, I felt ten times better having talked to him about my feelings.

A crooked smile grew on my face.

"Hey, Jamal, that's not all getting a period means."

"Yeah, what else does it mean?"

"It means my body is ready to make a baby. I'm practically a woman now," I bragged.

Jamal let out a hearty laugh. "So, who are you going to have this baby with—Sean Patterson?"

"Heck no," I said, pinching his arm. "Are you going to have a baby with Victoria Stevens?"

Jamal eyes got big and his cheesy smile went flat. "See— you know that's not funny. That girl is way too pushy."

Chapter 16

MY sixth grade year came to an end fast. And as predicted, I made the honor roll, Mama had chocolate chip cookies waiting for me on the last day of school, and I still wasn't boy crazy. Nothing really changed. Well—except for my bike. I had a new one now. I gave up my favorite Strawberry Shortcake bicycle for a much faster, bigger, red and black ten-speed. But, I wasn't ready to let go of everything just yet. Before Mama could give away my old bike, I took the basket off and fastened it to the front of my handlebars as a keepsake. Besides, Strawberry Shortcake and I went a long ways back. There was no way I could give her up cold turkey.

I was cruising down the newly laid asphalt on my street with my arms stretched wide open to let the wind run through my fingers. Smiling from ear to ear, I couldn't help being a daredevil—riding my bike with no hands. And of course, if Mama caught me, I'd get fussed at. But it was mid-July, after all, and the weather was perfect. I couldn't resist pedaling fast down the smooth black road that was just completed last month.

Mama still didn't have a good thing to say about the road expansion even though the traffic was much less than expected—a few more cars and trucks here and there but nothing consistent. Mama didn't care. She said there were a few more cars around here too many. The only way she'd allow me to ride my bike was if I learned hand signals and promise not to ride too fast.

I rolled into the grass and leaned my bike up against the side of the house. The strong scent of garlic hit my nose the moment I opened the screen door. It was spaghetti night. My mouth began to water as I walked toward the kitchen. Mama made the best homemade spaghetti with garlic bread. I hoped the food would be ready even though it was just a little after five o'clock.

"How long will it be until dinner is done?" I asked.

"Oh, not long," she replied, stirring a large pot. "I'm just finishing up with the sauce right now. And the noodles will only take a few minutes. Are you hungry?"

"Yes, ma'am," I answered, picking a cucumber out the salad bowl.

"Oh, no you don't!" Mama said, swatting me with a dishtowel. "You know better than to put your dirty hands on my food. Now, go get washed up for dinner."

I flashed Mama a guilty grin. "Yes, ma'am."

I turned around and bumped into Irene in the doorway. She had a smile on her face that was brighter than the sun.

"What are you so happy about?" I asked.

"Everything, sweetie—just everything."

"Well, don't hold it in, child. Tell us what's going on," Mama said.

Irene raised her hand, holding an envelope. "I did it." She beamed. "I got the fellowship to the University of Ghana. I'm going to Africa."

"Africa! You're going to Africa?" I blurted, shocked.

This was the first time I had ever heard Irene talk about going to school in another country—let alone Africa—where lions, tigers, and hyenas could eat her.

"Yes, Lovely, Africa! I'll be going there for historical research."

"Irene, what is all this?" Mama asked, sounding just as shocked as I was. "When were you going to tell us about this? Your father and I knew you wanted to go back to school to pursue your Ph.D. But we always thought you'd go somewhere nearby…not Africa."

"Well, I didn't want to say anything until I knew for sure." Irene sighed. "Oh, Mama, please don't be upset with me. You know I've always wanted to see the world and here's my chance to do it. Besides, this opportunity will only enhance my education career."

"But what about your job?" Mama asked.

"Don't worry. That's all been taken care of. The fellowship comes with a stipend. And I spoke with the principal a long time ago about this opportunity, and he was completely supportive and said I can resume my position when I return."

"Yeah, but you'll be so far away," I said slowly, processing this information. "Aren't you afraid?"

Irene lifted my chin and stared into my eyes. I had never seen her so happy before. "If you don't remember everything I tell you, remember this: Never give into fear. Because if you do, you'll become stuck in life and never grow."

"Well, I guess that's that," Mama said. "You've made your decision. So, when will you be leaving and how long will you be gone?"

"The program is for one year, and it starts in early September.

One year! I freaked out in my head.

Mama touched Irene's face. "I can't say that I'm happy to see you leave, but I sure am proud of you, baby. Congratulations on getting the fellowship."

"Thank you, Mama." Irene grinned; tears came to her eyes.

"Yeah, congratulations," I added, using a low voice.

"Oh, cheer up, Lovely. Don't sound so sad. One year will be over before you know it."

I flashed a fake smile. But secretly, I wasn't really happy for my sister at all. I just didn't want to see her leave. Irene turned and headed toward her bedroom.

"Hey, dinner's almost done. Aren't you gonna eat with us?" Mama asked.

"No," Irene shouted from her bedroom. "I'm meeting a friend for an early dinner at Quincy's."

Ooh, Quincy's. They have the best yeast rolls. "Can I come?" I yelled.

"Not this time, honey. Besides, I don't know what time I'll be getting back home."

Mama handed me a tray of food and iced tea. "Lovely, go take this to your dad. He wants to eat dinner in the den tonight."

Fifteen minutes later, Irene came back into the kitchen all dressed up with makeup on. She had on Jordache jeans with a dark purple short sleeve blouse and matching flats.

"Well, how do I look?" she asked, turning around.

"Wow! You look amazing," I said.

"Yes, you look beautiful, Irene—too beautiful to be going out with a girlfriend." Mama grinned. "Now, would you be going out with that young man you met at the teacher's convention last weekend?"

"Yes, ma'am, it actually is." She showed off another wide smile.

Ooh, I recognized Irene's smile. It was the kind you used when you like someone. I think Mama recognized it too.

"Well, you should bring him over so we can meet the man. And what's his name, again?"

"His name is Leonard, Mama. And we're just friends for now. That's why I'm meeting him for dinner. But, you never know." She shrugged. "He does have some promising qualities I like."

Irene gave me and Mama kisses. "I love you guys," she said, walking off. "And don't wait up."

Mama and I sat silently at the table with our thoughts. Only the sounds of our forks hitting plates could be heard. I pushed around the pile of spaghetti in front of me. After receiving Irene's news, it no longer seemed so appetizing.

"I can't believe she's moving to Africa for a year," I said, breaking the silence. "What am I going to do without her for an entire year?"

"Child, the same thing you're doing now," Mama replied. "You'll be just fine."

Then suddenly, we heard a loud noise. The most awful noise I had ever heard in my life.

I looked at Mama. Somehow I knew something was very wrong. My heart started to pound hard as I jumped away from the table and made a dash for the front door. I opened it.

"MAMA!" I screamed. "MAMA!"

Chapter 17

I heard someone say I hollered for over twenty minutes the day of the crash—that I was traumatized and kicked and screamed until Alvin picked me up and laid me on the living room couch. But I had no memory of that. All I remembered were the sights of Irene's lifeless body hanging out of the car and bright flashing lights.

A tractor trailer truck hit Irene's car head on. The driver fell asleep at the wheel and swerved into her lane at an estimated speed of 63 mph—killing Irene instantly. They said she didn't feel a thing.

The days after the accident were long and difficult. I had never faced death before. And I had never been so lost and lonely. The house felt cold without Irene, and I still couldn't bring myself to go into her room.

It was Sunday evening. We had the funeral two days earlier, and this was the first Sunday I had ever known us not to go to church. I guess Mama wasn't ready to be around a lot of people again. I knew I definitely wasn't.

The day of the funeral, our house was filled with food, flowers, and people wearing black. The news of Irene's death brought friends and family members from near and far. Even the mayor attended the service and gave Mama and Daddy his condolences in person. However, Ms. Lorraine saw the mayor's gesture differently. Back in the church yard, I heard her tell another woman that his words were just guilt talking because two days after the car crash, the town hall council held an emergency session and voted to reduce the speed limit on our street from 50 mph to 40 mph as well as put up yellow caution lights. "They could have done that from the beginning," she hissed.

By the large attendance, you could tell Irene was truly loved by many. But even though they meant well, I got tired of people hugging me and asking if I were all right. For some reason, that question made me uncomfortable. "Yes," I'd answer quickly with a nod, hoping to be left alone.

But Mama—she wasn't all right. She took Irene's death the hardest. Just the night before, while I was lying in my bed, I heard her crying and talking to Aunt Harriet in the kitchen. "Damn it," she cursed. "I told y'all that road was dangerous. Now my baby girl is gone."

It sounded like Mama's pain was unbearable, like someone had reached in deep and ripped her soul out. She went on to have several more outbursts like that—at least up until midnight, because that's when I couldn't listen anymore and had finally fallen asleep.

I had just started to comb my hair when I heard tapping at my window. I already knew who it was. "Jamal, you can't stay long, because I really don't feel like talking," I said, while helping him in.

"I know," he said, giving me a hug. "I hadn't heard from you since the funeral, so I got worried. Are you all right?"

There goes that darn question again.

"Yeah, I guess so," I answered, sitting down on the bed. "I've cried until I can't cry anymore. I just can't believe she's gone. "

"I know; it all seems so unreal." Jamal picked up my comb. "Were you combing your hair?"

"Yeah."

"Would you like for me to finish?"

I looked at him and nodded. "Sure."

Jamal stroked my hair several times and then started humming—just like Irene used to. His voice made me think of her and some of the good times we spent together, like playing dress-up and putting on makeup. I tried holding back my tears, but I couldn't. The memories were too strong. I leaned into Jamal's chest and began to sob, questioning why she had to go. I guess I wasn't all right after all. And I definitely wasn't all cried out.

I pulled away from Jamal. "Promise me you'll never leave. I've got to hear you say it."

He nodded. "I promise."

Part II

Chapter 18

Christmas Day 1986

MAMA asked me to cook Christmas dinner this year. After tasting my Thanksgiving pot roast last month, she praised and then gave my cooking skills her seal of approval. Nodding her head with a proud smile she said, "You're a quick learner, girlie, just like I was. You'll probably outdo me in the kitchen someday."

I took Mama's blessing to heart because I enjoyed preparing meals for the family. After Irene died, it was like something inside me changed. I felt less like a little kid. I felt more compelled to take care of my parents. So I decided to learn how to cook by watching and imitating Mama's every move in the kitchen. Sure, the work was hard sometimes— cooking and cleaning up everyday when I could have been doing teenage things. But I understood my new role. And knew I needed to help out around the house as much as I could—especially since the Parkinson's disease was affecting Daddy's mobility even more these days and had added extra work on Mama, which tired her out easily.

Ever since Daddy's walking slowed down to a snail's pace, things became more difficult. And that became a huge problem. Mainly because it made it hard for him to get to the bathroom fast enough to handle his own business. Many times, he had accidents. And too many times, Mama had to clean up those accidents. That's why he's been wearing adult diapers for over a year now. But we looked on the brighter side of things...at least his mind wasn't gone.

Mama could have hired a nurse to help out with Daddy's needs a couple of times a week from the settlement she received in Irene's wrongful death suit. But she chose not to. She said $105,000 may seem like a lot of money, but after paying off Irene's student loans, lawyer's fees, and Daddy's medical expenses, it really wasn't much. But she did buy a new burgundy Ford Taurus and gave our old 1977 Chevrolet Caprice to Aunt Harriet because they had been without a working car for some time. The rest of the money went into savings and toward my college fund.

I decided to go simple for dinner—just some baked chicken, white rice, candied yams, and black-eyed peas from a can. Mama took on the homemade pie and cake because I hadn't begun to master baking yet. The only thing I could do was put store bought cookie dough on a sheet of waxed paper and turn on the oven...which suited me just fine.

We planned on having a quiet Christmas dinner because we went all out for Thanksgiving. I set the table for just a few. Aunt Harriet and Cynthia were over—but Addie, her husband, and Deidra were away for the holidays. Even Jamal was out of town.

Dinner was ready to serve. When I walked into the den to put food on the table, I saw Aunt Harriet peeking behind the curtains. Then I watched her move to the other side of the window and do the same thing.

What is she doing? I walked around the table dropping ice cubes in cups.

"Aunt Harriet, what are you looking for?" I finally said.

She gave me a backward glance. "You'll see in a few minutes," she said excitedly.

I looked at Cynthia. "What's going on?" I mouthed.

She came closer to my ear and whispered, "It's a surprise for Aunt Dolores."

"A surprise," I repeated. "Well, what is it? I can keep a secret."

"Nope, can't do it." She shook her head. "You'll just have to find out with everyone else. Besides, Mama made me promise not to tell a soul."

"Are you serious? You're really not going to tell me?"

"No." She chuckled.

"Fine," I scoffed. "Don't tell me. But I hope this gift gets here soon because dinner is on the table and I'm hungry."

I turned toward Daddy.

"Daddy!" I shouted so his deafening ears could hear. "Are you ready to eat?"

"I sure am," he answered, perking up in his recliner.

As I headed to get Mama from her bedroom, I flashed Cynthia a disapproving look, still not understanding why she and Aunt Harriet couldn't trust me with their mysterious gift. I took another glimpse of Aunt Harriet. She was still gazing out of the window like a watch guard...waiting.

***

"You did a wonderful job, Lovely," Mama said. "Everything you made was very tasty."

"It sure was," Aunt Harriet agreed as she reached over for a second slice of sweet potato pie. "Little Miss Lovely is turning out to be a real homemaker—taking on all these house duties.

Now, if I could only get Cynthia to do more cooking for us, I'd be a happier old woman."

Aunt Harriet started to laugh, but Cynthia was not amused.

"Well, not all of us are cut out to be a Betty Crocker, Mama."

"Maybe not," Aunt Harriet snapped back. But...I bet, if you wanted to, you could learn how to cook. Just like you learned how to fix your hair and put all that makeup on your face."

Cynthia rolled her eyes as she looked away.

"And don't be cutting your eyes at me, young lady. They were very nasty," Aunt Harriet said.

The sound of a car door slamming broke the tension in the air.

"Who could that be this time of night?" Mama asked.

Aunt Harriet sprung up. "I'll find out who it is. You just sit right there."

I leaned into Cynthia and whispered, "What's going on with you and Aunt Harriet?"

Cynthia rolled her eyes again. Luckily, her mama wasn't here to see it.

"Oh, girl, nothing. She's just mad because I'm not going to college. I really don't see the problem. I mean, she didn't go to college and she turned out fine as a seamstress."

"Dolores, look who I found at the door."

Mama turned around.

"Surprise!" Aunt Harriet shouted, standing arm-in-arm with a man who wore a black leather cap and a jacket that had a lot of military patches on it.

Mama's eyes grew big. Then, slowly, she rose to her feet and walked over to the man. This man I'd never seen before in my life apparently was no stranger to Mama. She took her hands and placed them on his cheeks. Looking pleased, she asked, "Nathan Glover, where have you been?"

"Just about everywhere, sister," he answered, grinning.

"That's our uncle?" I shot into Cynthia's ear. "But he looks so much younger than them."

"Yep," she replied.

"Long time, no see—young man," Daddy said.

"Hey, Mr. Joseph. It's good to see you too."

"Boy, look at you. I haven't seen you in years…you look good. Now come here and give your old sister a hug."

After a few seconds, Mama pulled away with her hands still clutching his arm. "Did you drive here? We heard a car."

"Oh, no ma'am," he said. "I took a cab from the Greyhound bus station."

Mama turned to Aunt Harriet. "You knew he was coming today, didn't you?"

"Yes, ma'am," she admitted. "Ever since last month when he called. And, chil', you have no idea how hard it was for me to keep this secret from you."

"Trust me, Aunt Dolores," Cynthia jumped in. "I know exactly how hard it was. There were so many times she wanted to get on the phone and spill the beans, but she restrained herself."

"You said Aunt Dolores." Nathan pointed his finger. "Then you must be Cynthia."

Cynthia nodded her head with a smile. "Hello, Uncle Nathan."

"Girl, the last time I saw you, you were barely a knee high. Now, look atcha. You're all grown up and beautiful."

Cynthia's eyes lit up like a flame on a torch. Even I could see she was blushing through her dark chocolate skin. "Thank you," she replied sweetly.

That's when my new uncle turned his attention to me.

"So that means you, young lady, must be Lovely. And, my goodness—what a fitting name. Now, I've never seen you in the flesh, sweetheart. But I do remember your baby picture Irene sent me many years ago."

The smile on my face melted when he mentioned Irene's name. "It's nice to meet you, sir."

Uncle Nathan seemingly understood my reaction. He gave me a nod and then looked back at Mama. I could tell her tight-lipped smile masked her ongoing grief even though it had been almost two years since Irene's death.

"Oh, Dolores, I am so sorry about Irene. I truly am. I didn't find out about her passing until I called Harriet. I was devastated. That's why I got back here as soon as I could."

"It's all right, baby," Mama said, still smiling as a single tear trickled down her face. "We're taking it one day at a time and trusting in the Lord. But, you must know, we wanted to contact you. We just didn't know how."

Uncle Nathan blew out a long sigh. "I know, Dolores. It's not your fault. I've moved so many times over the years—trying to get my life together. Y'all would of never found me. But I'm hoping all of that is going to change real soon."

"So how long are you here for?" Aunt Harriet asked.

"I think for a while...if you'll have me."

"Oh, boy, don't be silly," Mama replied. You're family. You can stay as long as you like. Listen, just give me a few minutes and I'll have Irene's old room all freshened up for you."

"Oh, that won't be necessary, Dolores," Aunt Harriet said, shaking her head. "I've got a room already set up for him across the street. Our baby bother will be staying with me and Cynthia. Besides, it'll be nice to have a man around the house again."

Mama chuckled then said, "Well, you heard your sister; sounds like she's got it all planned out. But I don't care where you sleep, Nathan. I'm just happy to have you home."

Chapter 19

"A broken soul trying to make himself whole again" was how Cynthia explained Uncle Nathan's longtime absence. At least that's what Aunt Harriet told her. They said Uncle Nathan was a deeply wounded man—physically *and* emotionally scarred from his service in the Vietnam War. When he returned from the war in 1970, he barely spoke a word, drank too much, and barricaded himself in his bedroom. And then, one day, he just disappeared…leaving behind most of his stuff and a note saying, *I can't stay here. I've gotta leave.*

That note was written sixteen years ago.

I also found out that Aunt Harriet, with the help of Mama, raised Uncle Nathan. Unfortunately, a few years after his birth, their mother died from a sudden death, transforming their baby brother into something like a son—a son they hadn't seen in years. The only contact he made was by a rare letter or phone call just to let his sisters know he was alive. So their tearful reunion made sense.

At the age of forty-five, Uncle Nathan stood about six feet tall, medium built, and walked with a slight limp. The limp came from a bullet that shattered a bone in his right leg and got him medically discharged from the army. He had no children, no wife. And for over a decade, he'd been living life like a gypsy—completely free to travel the country as he saw fit and make his home wherever his head lay. There was even talk that he got as far as California to do some protesting with the Black Panthers. Maybe that's what inspired that black leather cap he liked to wear.

But whatever problems he had in the past, they must've been long gone, because he didn't seem sad to me at all. Uh, uh—no way! That's because Uncle Nathan smiled all the time and often had something funny to say. To me, he was a welcomed change. Ever since his arrival last Christmas, it was like a dark veil had been lifted off our house, and it was filled with joy and laughter again. Even Mama's spirits were up and her broken heart appeared to be on the mend.

***

Saturday, April 11, 1987. The day was warm, sunny, and we were celebrating my parents' forty-seventh wedding anniversary. Mama didn't want to make a fuss, but Uncle Nathan insisted we have a cookout, a party or something— anything to commemorate such a huge milestone. "It ain't like anniversaries like these come around often," he repeated until Mama finally caved in and settled on having a small cookout serving the usual food with the usual people attending, well— except for Cynthia. The moment she got her cosmetology license and a new job at some hair salon in the next town over, we started seeing less of her. Cynthia claimed she had to work today and couldn't stay for dinner. But, before she ditched us, she made sure to pay her respects by dropping off an anniversary card and a lemon glazed pound cake she bought from a store.

The party was low key. There weren't a lot of people or loud music playing in the background like we used to have. But that didn't stop Uncle Nathan from dancing in the yard like it was 1999. I mean the man was dancing all by his lonesome with his eyes shut while he wiggled his shoulders and hips. I didn't know what he was doing. And I'm sure he didn't know either. Maybe those strange dance moves and extra energy came from the tall can of beer he had in his hand. Several times, he even held it closely to his chest as though it were a dance partner.

"It looks like your uncle is having a good time. Do you think he's drunk?" Jamal asked.

"Not sure." I shrugged. "I've never seen him drunk before."

"Has he even found a job yet?"

"Nope…I think he stopped looking."

Surprisingly, Jamal showed up to the cookout. I was surprised because he had declined a few other dinner invitations I had given him in recent months. He had a new interest in life, something he enjoyed more than food and hanging out with me: his trumpet.

Jamal started playing the trumpet in the sixth grade and then joined the jazz band in the seventh. At first, it was just something to do. But all of a sudden, in our last semester of middle school, he'd been taking his instrument pretty seriously, which meant spending less time with me and a lot more time practicing with his band mate, Quincy McNeil, who also played the trumpet.

Without whining or sounding like a nagging girlfriend, I kinda let him know he was missed. I mean, I knew I definitely wasn't his girlfriend, and we had our own friends, but I missed our daily phone calls and our occasional walks to the corner store.

Jamal asked me not to take it personal because he really liked playing the trumpet and wanted to join the high school marching band next fall. And maybe, with luck, even win a music scholarship to college. But all of those things required practicing a lot and earning first chair. I told him I understood even though, secretly, I felt we were drifting apart.

"So, how's practice going?" I asked while stretching my legs. I had been sitting on the steps for thirty minutes and my knees were going numb.

"Ah, it's going okay."

"Just okay!" I gave him a puzzled glimpse. "You should be state champion as much as you practice."

"I know, right." Jamal snickered then took a bite of his hotdog. "So guess what?"

"What?"

"I'm trying out for a spot in the marching band next week."

"Oh really, so soon? Is Quincy trying out for the marching band too?"

"Yeah, he is."

"Now, wouldn't he be like competition?"

"I guess so, but I'm sure we'll both get in. Most of the trumpet players in the band right now are seniors, and they'll be graduating in June...so." Jamal tipped his cup up to his mouth and then started chomping on ice.

"So what did you get on Mrs. Kimble's math test?" he asked.

"I got an A. What about you?"

"I got a B."

"Well, that's not bad."

"Yeah, but I didn't beat you." He smiled.

"Ha!" I snickered. "Good luck with that one."

"So what's going on with you lately? Are you and Sabrina still bowling?"

"Yeah, we went last weekend. It was fun," I said then mumbled, "Too bad you weren't there."

"And down he goes," Jamal said, like an announcer at a boxing match.

"Who's down?" I asked, turning my head.

And sure enough, it was Uncle Nathan lying on his back like a bug with its limbs in the air—laughing and rocking back and forth trying to get on his feet. Yep, without a doubt, he was drunk.

Chapter 20

ANIKA'S last performance at Mt. Moriah Baptist church ended with thunderous applause. Some people even wept and rose to their feet because they were so moved. But the woman sitting next to me said, "My *God* that girl can sing. If I had a wig on, I'd snatch it off and run around this church."

Anika told me her father was offered a job. He accepted an executive position with the City of Atlanta's waste management system. The position meant more money, of course, but it also meant Anika would get the opportunity to attend a prestigious high school for the arts, which could also get her into Spellman College...her mother's dream college.

I dreaded a long, emotional goodbye with Anika, so when she walked me to my car, I just gave her a hug, smiled, and said, "See you later." Anika also played it cool. She replied by giving me a head nod and a cheeky smile. Staring back at each other, we both knew this day would come—the day when Anika would, eventually, move on to bigger and better things. That's why we didn't cry, because we also knew we'd see each other again someday. After all, some of her family still lived in the area.

Looking out the window as we drove home, I couldn't help but think about the loneliness I was going to face this summer now that Anika was gone. Jamal would be at band camp during the day, and I wouldn't have anyone to talk to at church. And that's when it really hit me, as we passed by patches of purple horsemint weed along the roadside, how much I had already missed Anika. Besides being entertained by her voice and creative hairstyles, she was the one I told all my girly secrets to: like how I felt the night I got my period, my first dance with a boy, and when I kissed Jamal. Who could possibly take her place? And then I thought about it—at least I still had fast-talking, boy-crazy Sabrina to call. Sure, I could never get a word in over the phone, but at least she was still in my area code.

The moment I got home, I peeled off my dress and then replaced it with one of Mama's old muumuus to clean up and start dinner. Funny, thing though. I thought I wouldn't be caught dead in one of these dresses. But, now that I was older, I understood their appeal. They were so light and airy and easy to cook in. Not only that, they also covered up the big butt I inherited from my birth mother. And I noticed mine had gotten a little bigger ever since I stopped riding my bike on a normal basis and switched to eating junk food and reading books in my bedroom all day.

I whipped up some meatloaf, homemade mashed potatoes, and green beans instead of the typical baked macaroni and cheese with chicken or roast we'd eat on a Sunday evening after church. I felt like doing something different. Everything else was changing around me, so why not also change what we ate each day of the week?

A couple hours later, Mama came into the kitchen sniffing. "Girl, whatever you've got cooking on the stove smells good to me."

"Thank you, Mama," I said and then told her what was on the menu.

The screen door slammed shut.

"I smell tomato sauce. What are you cooking, Lovely?" Aunt Harriet asked.

"Meatloaf and mashed potatoes."

"Is it done yet?"

I nodded. "Yes ma'am."

"Well, hurry up and fix me a plate," Aunt Harriet ordered as she sat down at the table. "And go ahead and fix your uncle a plate too because he's not feeling too well. I doubt he'll be coming over to eat tonight."

"What's wrong with Nathan?" Mama asked.

"Chil', I really don't know. All I know he was lying in bed and staring at TV with sweat rolling down his face when I checked on him last."

"That sounds like he's got the flu or something. But it's the middle of May," Mama pointed out. "Well, does he have a fever? Better yet, maybe we should just take 'em to the emergency room and get him checked out?"

"Now, I don't know anything about a fever. But, I did tell him he should see a doctor about getting some medicine. Then he told me he already took his medicine and was waiting for it to kick in."

"Okay, good," Mama said, sounding relieved. "Then he should be able to sleep it off."

I set down a plate in front of Aunt Harriet, and she wasted no time taking a bite of my meatloaf.

"Mmm, mmm! This is delicious."

After three more bites, Aunt Harriet got up and went to the stove to put another piece of meatloaf on her plate. "Listen, baby," she said, smacking, "go ahead and take that plate over to Nathan, because I see I'm gonna be at this table for a while."

"Yes ma'am," I said, reaching for a takeout tray on top of the refrigerator. "Should I take a plate for Cynthia too?"

"Oh, no, honey," she said quickly. "Miss Cynthia isn't home. She just went somewhere with her male friend."

"What male friend?" Mama asked.

"I don't know, Dolores. She just called him a friend as she scurried on out the front door. But I know this much: Cynthia better not come back to my house pregnant or at an inappropriate hour. I don't care how grown she thinks she is."

Chapter 21

I walked into Aunt Harriet's dark house and looked around. The only light I could see down the hall was from the hood above the stove in the kitchen. "Uncle Nathan," I called out, passing through the living room.

"Back here," he replied.

I stood in his doorway. The light was off, but I could see him lying in bed watching television. "It's me, Uncle Nathan. Aunt Harriet said you weren't feeling well. So I brought over some dinner I cooked."

"Oh, I'm feeling much better now." He began to sit up in bed. "Do me a favor and turn on the light for me."

When I turned on the light I saw that Uncle Nathan did not have on a shirt, but his bottom half was covered with a sheet. Instantly, my head turned away but I still wondered if he were naked underneath.

"Thanks for the food, Lovely, let's see what you got."

Quickly, I moved to the side of the bed and set the tray on his lap. With a closer view, I noticed he had tattoos of an eagle, two guns, and the word *Army* on his muscular arms and chest. Surprisingly, Uncle Nathan looked pretty strong for a man who was considered disabled.

After flashing a smile, I turned around and walked away just as fast toward the door. I guess I felt more uncomfortable with him being topless than I expected.

"Hey!" he said with a chuckle. "Where are you going so fast? Don't you wanna know what I think of your food?"

I stopped then looked back to see him opening the box for a taste. His eyes closed.

"Mmm," he moaned then pointed at me. "I know I've told you this before, but you really can cook. Actually, your meatloaf is better than Dolores'. But don't tell her I said that."

Uncle Nathan took another bite and nodded in approval. "And how old are you again?"

"Thirteen," I answered, showing off a shy, yet proud smile.

"Girl, I'm telling you—with your cooking skills, you'll never have a problem finding a husband. But, wait," he said, wearing a smirk. "You already got a husband—don't you?"

"I have? Who?" I asked, clueless.

"Oh, girl, don't play dumb with me. You know exactly who I'm talking about," he said, lifting his fork again.

"Are you talking about Jamal?"

"Of course I am." He chewed. "They tell me you two have been inseparable for years…like two peas in a pod."

"No, really, Uncle Nathan," I laughed. "Jamal and I are just friends. We don't even look at each other like that."

"Well, maybe not now. But just wait until those hormones kick in. I'll give it another few months to a year—then you'll see." Uncle Nathan wiped his mouth and then pointed to the dresser. "Pass me that soda, darling."

I handed him the warm Pepsi bottle.

"Do you want some ice?"

"Nah, this will do just fine," he answered, taking a swig. "Ahhh—that hit the spot."

Uncle Nathan took a few more gulps and bobbed his head. "Yep, just a little while longer and Jamal will be chasing you like a dog after a cat. And if he doesn't, well, something's wrong with him—because from what I'm seeing, you're going to be a looker, just like your mother."

I lowered my eyes with a smile. I felt flattered by his compliment but embarrassed at the same time. "Thank you," I said. And that's when his words came back to me. I took a seat on the end of the bed. "Uncle Nathan...you knew my birth mother?"

"Sure, I met Corinne once, when I came home on a short leave from the army. The family threw me a dinner party and she showed up with Irene."

Suddenly, he started laughing.

"What's so funny?" I asked.

"Oh, I'm just remembering how shy Corinne was. That girl was so shy—she could barely make eye contact with me or anyone else for that matter."

When Uncle Nathan stopped laughing, he took another sip of his soda and placed the bottle on the nightstand. "But behind all that shyness and plain-Jane clothing," he continued, "anybody could see Corinne was a fine woman. And, man, could she sing."

"She could sing?"

"Yes, ma'am!" he exclaimed. "Irene didn't tell you?"

"No, sir." I shook my head.

"Well, it was like pulling teeth at first, but when Irene finally convinced her to sing in front of all of us at that party, man—it was like listening to a songbird. In hindsight, I truly believe that was the moment Corinne started to come out of her shell, because soon after that, I received several letters from Irene telling me how Corinne was singing everywhere with a R&B band and shaking a tail feather in tight sequin dresses."

My birth mother is a singer…wow!

"Now, the question is, young lady…can you sing?"

"Oh, no sir, that talent skipped me."

"Now ain't that something," he said. "Cynthia told me the same thing."

"So you and Irene were close?"

"Yes, ma'am," he answered. "I was more like a brother to her than an uncle. Irene told me everything. As a matter of fact"—he snickered—"I'm the second person she told about her secret marriage."

"Secret marriage!" I repeated in shock.

Instantly, an *Oh, crap!* look appeared on Uncle Nathan's face.

"I guess Irene and Dolores didn't tell you about that either," he said. Well, how about we just keep that between the two of us, okay?"

"Don't worry, uncle. I won't say a thing. But I can't believe Irene was once married."

"Oh, yes, Irene ran off and married her high school sweetheart—Gavin Wells. They were something like you and Jamal…inseparable. But, unfortunately, the marriage was short-lived."

My eyes widened. "Why?"

"Well, poor Gavin died from a sudden heart attack during basketball camp in college. They said he had some kind of heart defect that went undetected."

"Oh my God, that's awful."

"Yeah, it sure was tragic and very painful for Irene. I reckon that's the reason no one ever told you about it."

I nodded. "And I bet it's also the reason why she never used his last name."

"Exactly. That's why I was so glad Irene had Corinne for comfort. I was too busy fighting a war."

"Irene and Corinne were really close, huh?"

"Of course, who do think Irene told first about the marriage?"

I walked out of Aunt Harriet's house intrigued by what Uncle Nathan had revealed about Corinne and Irene. Corinne, the singer, was no longer an old black and white photograph in a book. She had a story. And Irene's scandalous marriage made me wonder what other secrets were hidden in the family. With these revelations, I felt like I was living in one of my mystery books. I couldn't get curiosity off my brain.

Chapter 22

SITTING in math class, I felt a pinch on my shoulder blade that made me twitch. I turned around quick with narrowed eyes. "Why did you pull my bra strap?" I asked Jamal.

"I just wanted to snap you out of your daze." He laughed. "What are you thinking about so hard anyway?"

"Nothing," I replied.

"Don't give me that, girl. I've known you long enough to know when something's on your mind...especially when you're staring out of the window instead of paying attention to the teacher."

"Really, Jamal, it's nothing," I whispered.

"Lovely," Mrs. Kimble called out, "would you like to share with the class what you and Jamal are talking about?"

"No ma'am." I shook my head.

"All right then, please stop talking in my class."

"Yes ma'am," I mumbled.

A few minutes later, I slipped Jamal a note: *I'll tell you later.*

***

The second I got on the bus I heard the Stanley sisters bragging about their farewell to middle school pool party next weekend. They promised the entire eighth grade class it would be a party to remember with unlimited food, games, and even a live DJ on site. And, of course, they just had to boast about having one of the biggest underground swimming pools in all of Willisburg. No doubt the sisters would make good on their claims—after all, they came from money.

Their father was Dr. Stanley, a successful second-generation dentist in the community, who had a reputation of spoiling his daughters, which made them rotten to the core. Truth be told, nobody really liked the Stanley sisters. That's why they often had to buy their friendships with parties and stuff.

Before sitting down, I reached into my book bag to fish out a candy bar.

"Hey, Lovely," Jessica Stanley shouted from the back of the bus, "are you coming to my pool party?"

I looked up and saw Jessica's excited blue eyes and expectant grin. Ever since I gave her a compliment on her penny loafers and plaid skirt last year, it seemed like she thought of me as either a friend or a fan. I forced a smile on my face and then lied, "I probably will. Thanks for the invitation." I knew lying was wrong. But, I didn't have the heart to burst her bubble in front of her sister and rented friends.

Just as I started chewing my candy bar, I heard my name being called again. This time, it was Jamal. "Slide over," he whispered, putting my book bag on the floor. "I searched for you during lunch but you were nowhere to be found."

"I was in the library reading."

"The entire lunch period?" He grimaced.

" I needed peace and quiet to finish my book. You know reading is a good thing, Jamal...you should try it."

"Whatever," he said then eagle-eyed my candy bar.

I gave him stern look. "One bite, Jamal...I mean it."

Dang it! I shrieked in my head.

I should have known better than to trust that boy with some food because the second I gave him permission, he shot me a devious grin then took a huge bite of my candy bar— leaving behind only a smidge of chocolate for me to eat.

I rammed my elbow straight into his arm. "You dirty jerk!"

"Ow!" he yelped then started rubbing his arm. "You said one bite."

I rolled my eyes hard to make sure he knew I was pissed. "You play too much."

And that's when Jamal did something he'd never done before. He slid his arm across my back and caressed my shoulder. "Don't be mad at me, Lovely," he said lowly, close to my ear. "I'm sorry."

And just that fast, the sound of Jamal's newly deepened voice and his touch sent a surge of warmth throughout my body I'd never felt before. Not even the short-lived crushes I had on Sean Patterson or Barry Ultman made me feel this way. It was like I had gotten zapped with a jolt of electricity and it went straight to my pants.

Is this what Uncle Nathan warned me about? Or what Aunt Harriet meant when she called Cynthia hot in the behind?

"Why are you riding the bus anyway?" I asked, trying to shake off the unusual sensation. "I thought you had after-school band practice today."

"Oh, I'm done for now." He pulled away his arm. "I don't have to attend practice again until marching band camp starts up next month. Anyway, what did you want to tell me earlier?"

I heard Jamal talking but it all sounded faint in the background while I tried to work out my feelings. *Me and Jamal? No way!* I chuckled in my head. For years we'd been telling people that we were just friends. We couldn't, all of a sudden, be girlfriend and boyfriend...right?

"Lovely," he repeated, finally catching my attention.

"What?"

"There you go again—doing that thing you do."

"What thing?" I asked.

"Zoning out! Look, what did you have to tell me?"

"Oh, yeah, guess what I found out from Uncle Nathan yesterday?"

"What?"

"First, Irene got married at age eighteen but then her husband died. And secondly, my birth mother was a singer."

"A singer?" he asked, wide-eyed. "Like a famous singer from back in the day?"

"No, boy. Wait...he never said. I don't think so."

Jamal started laughing. "Too bad you didn't get her gift because I've heard your singing and..." He stopped talking and began shaking his head.

"Shut up." I laughed along, knowing he was right.

"But seriously Jamal, now I'm starting to wonder what else I don't know about my birth mother. And why didn't Irene tell me she was a singer?"

"Well, it sounds like your uncle knew your birth mother. Maybe he knows why Irene kept stuff from you."

"He said he only met her once."

"Yeah, but maybe he knows more than you think."

"Maybe." I shrugged.

While looking at Jamal's face, I started to see things I never noticed before. Like his eyes turned light brown in the sunlight, he had nice teeth and peach fuzz for a mustache. And just like that, those questions came back to me like a boomerang. Then I had another thought: What if Jamal had feelings for me but was too afraid to say? I wanted to know, so I started chuckling to bring up the subject.

"What are you laughing about?" he asked, falling right into my script.

"Well, you wanna hear something funny?"

"Sure, I'm up for a good joke."

"Get this…Uncle Nathan also said that you and I are going to get married in the future. What do you think of that?"

At first, Jamal gave me a blank stare then he burst into laughter.

"So now your uncle is a psychic? Are you sure he wasn't drunk? I mean, we're just friends. Did you tell him, Lovely? We're just friends, right?"

"Ha. Ha. Ha…yeah! That's what I told him."

Even though I said that out loud, in my head, I was thinking something totally different. A part of me was relieved that Jamal and I got that weird conversation out of the way and it confirmed Jamal wasn't into me.

But I have to admit, a small part of me felt disappointed because—deep down inside—I kind of liked that warm feeling he gave me.

Chapter 23

UNDERNEATH Mama's oversized sunhat, I dug around in the soil to finish planting this year's wildflower seeds in the flowerbeds below the front porch. I sowed some bluish-purple lupines and cornflowers to complement the mustard-colored sunflowers and white Shasta daisies that were already in full bloom. It amazed me how, just a few years ago, I couldn't distinguish one flower from the other or plant a single vegetable, but now I could recite names and types. And my thumb was getting greener with each passing year. All thanks to Mama, of course.

Mama didn't feel like working in the yard this morning. She said her knees had been giving her some problems lately and there was no way she could get on the ground and crawl around in the dirt. But she potted some fresh African violets and positioned them on the sides of the front door in memory of Irene. African Violets were Irene's favorite and potting those flowers has become Mama's ritual for two summers now.

"Aunt Dolores," I heard behind me.

I turned around and looked up. "Cynthia, it's me."

"Lovely, what are you wearing?" she asked, twisting her mouth in disapproval. "I thought you were Aunt Dolores."

I stood up and dusted off my blue and white-checkered housecoat. "What? This is comfortable."

Cynthia continued to scan me over with her judgmental eyes and then shook her head.

"Girl, you're gonna make yourself old before you ever become young. Go put some shorts on! Show some shape! Better yet, why don't you find a summer school activity, like Jamal? You should be hanging around kids your own age instead of dressing like an old lady."

By the tone of Cynthia's voice, I already knew she was in one of her funky moods that had nothing to do with me or my choice of clothing. Standing there in jean shorts with her arms folded over, she wore a plastic cap on her head along with a stained towel around her neck. Obviously, she was dying her hair again. Last month it was light brown and now it looked like she was going back to black. I had no idea why she was here so early, getting on my nerves. But I just wanted her to shut up and leave me alone. And I knew exactly how to do it.

"Cynthia, you're right. I should join a summer school activity, especially if you agree to help Mama get Daddy to the toilet every morning while I'm gone."

Yep, that did the trick.

The moment I brought up housework, Cynthia's mouth zipped. A crazed look appeared on her face instead. I gloated inside, watching her squirm. But then I changed the subject to let her off the hook. "I see you're changing your hair color again."

"I'm trying to." She sounded annoyed. "But Mama kept on bugging me to come over here to get some washing powder. Like she couldn't wait until I finished my hair. Honestly, I don't understand why she couldn't send Uncle

Nathan. He wasn't doing anything. All he does is eat, sleep, shit, and watch television in his room all day. If I didn't have a job, she'd be on my case."

"Well, at least we have mothers to get on our nerves," I said.

"Oh, no." She shook her head. "Not you too. Mama gives me enough reminders on how lucky I am. So I don't need you to be her parrot, okay. Besides, I'm tired of being overly grateful—I didn't ask to be here."

And that's where Cynthia and I saw things differently. I couldn't thank my parents enough for giving me the Duval name.

"Speaking of Uncle Nathan," I said, changing the subject yet again, "did he tell you that Corinne was a singer?"

Cynthia sucked her teeth. "He mentioned it. But I already knew that."

"You did?"

"Yeah." She shrugged. "What about it?"

"Doesn't that make you want to know more about her— or even meet her?"

"Hell no!" Cynthia's face wrinkled into a grimace. "That woman abandon us. She could be singing on stage with Aretha Franklin for all I care."

"Well, I do wonder about her. I wonder if she's still singing in a band or if she's even alive."

"Oh, trust me. Corinne Scott is alive and kicking somewhere. She's probably living in Batesville County, near her parents. And that's just three hours away."

"See, I didn't even know that."

"And now you know everything I know. Well, except the fact that her parents didn't want us either."

"That can't be true."

"Sure it is," she asserted. "Mama told me everything. She told me how Corinne betrayed Irene by not keeping her word to visit just to go on tour with a band and how her parents turned their backs on us during each adoption." Cynthia snickered. "But here's the kicker. Knowing all of this, I still sent our so-called grandparents a Christmas card one year— even drew a heart inside. And guess what they did... They sent the damn thing back with *Return to Sender* written across the envelope. So I'm telling you, Lovely, the Scott family wants nothing to do with us. And tracking down Corinne will only bring you disappointment and hurt in the end."

"Why didn't y'all tell me any of this?" I asked.

"Maybe we wanted to spare you. It wouldn't of made a difference anyway."

I shrugged. "I'm still curious, Cynthia. Maybe Corinne isn't as bad as her parents. I could talk to Mama about reaching out to Corinne, but I don't want to upset her. Maybe I should just ask Uncle Nathan to help me. After all, he did meet her once. And who knows, all of this might lead to meeting our birth father. "

With a sigh, Cynthia finally dropped the attitude and spoke to me with a softer tone.

"Listen, Lovely. If you want to start searching around for Corinne, well—that's your choice. But, please, leave Uncle Nathan out of it. He may seem cool and all, but there's something not right about him. I don't trust him and neither should you."

"You don't trust him? Why?"

"Well, for one thing, the man's a leech. He borrowed five dollars from me last month and hasn't paid me back yet, and secondly, I don't like the way he watches me. Just gives me the creeps."

"Okay." I nodded, not knowing what else to say.

"Look, let me go get this washing powder because my scalp is starting to sting."

Cynthia walked off but then gave me a backward glance. "Remember what I said."

As I squatted to pick up the gardening tools and supplies, I really didn't know what to make of Cynthia's warnings. I couldn't get Corinne out of my mind. And the way I saw it, Uncle Nathan never acted strange around me. So why should I treat him any differently?

I heard a lawnmower being revved up. It was Alvin from next door. Nowadays he'd been sporting a bushy beard. But he still loved wearing that rundown orange Clemson T-shirt which I doubted he'd ever give up. We made eye contact so I gave him a wave and a quick smile. And, as usual, his smile was bigger than life—and always making him appear like the happiest man on the earth.

Chapter 24

ON her day off, Cynthia was more than happy to drive Jamal and me to Sabrina's fourteenth birthday party at the skating rink. As a matter of fact, back at the house, she even volunteered to fix my hair—something she'd only done a few times before. I found it kind of suspicious. Why the sudden interest in me when she normally kept to herself and out of my business?

Cynthia braided my hair into a jumbo cornrow with a neatly trimmed front bang. Then she persuaded me to wear her yellow hoop earrings along with her yellow slip shoes to match my royal blue jeans and off-the-shoulder top. I grudgingly agreed to wear those hoops because I never liked big earrings. There was just something about the way they knocked up against my cheek I found annoying. But she lectured me on trying out new things while putting a reddish gloss on my lips, something else I never wore.

After dressing me up to her standards, Cynthia stood behind me and placed her hands on my shoulders. "See—this is what a teenager is supposed to look like," she said, gazing into the bathroom mirror. I stared at myself pleasantly surprised. I actually looked stylish like Sabrina.

When we picked up Jamal, he had the same stunned reaction. From the backseat, he said, "You really look nice tonight, Lovely." I said thanks then turned my head, trying to hide my blushing smile, but Cynthia saw and gave me a nudge with her elbow.

The moment Jamal and I entered the building together, I felt like all eyes were on us with so many heads turning from different directions. Sabrina stood up from a long table decorated with pink and green balloons and started waving as we walked toward her. She looked amazing, beaming in a denim-blue acid washed overall with multi-colored scrunches in her hair and bangles to match on her wrist.

A lot of people showed up for Sabrina's party, which wasn't a shock. With her outgoing, magnetic personality, she was bound to have plenty of friends. A few girls and boys I knew from school. But the other kids, I didn't know. I gave Sabrina my gift, although Jamal's name was added to the card. He claimed forgetting to buy his own.

"Happy birthday, Sabrina! I love your outfit," I said.

With wide eyes, Sabrina set the box down next to a pile of other gifts.

"Oh my God, Lovely! You look good too!" she squealed, giving Jamal and me a hug. "And I love what you've done to your hair."

Just when she said that, I caught some girl cutting her eyes at me.

"Thank you," I replied, sounding confident and not giving that girl another thought.

***

After about an hour of skating and repeatedly busting our butts from falling down, Sabrina and I left everybody behind to go back to the table and rest. Three of Sabrina's girlfriends, which I learned were from her dance club, were already there talking—including Dawn, the one who gave me the evil look.

"Hey, what are y'all talking about?" Sabrina asked.

"Who else? My boyfriend, of course," Dawn said.

"What about him?"

"Well, we're going to different schools in the fall, and I may meet someone new. So I need to find a way to dump him."

"Why don't you just break it off over the phone?" Sabrina chuckled. "Isn't that what you normally do?"

"Yeah, I tried that. But he keeps calling me and asking for another chance. He's like a needy stray cat that won't go away." Dawn sighed. "I knew I should have never let him put a hickey on my boob."

Everyone laughed, except for me. I was too shocked from what I heard. And Dawn noticed.

"What? You seem surprised, Lovely. Surely you've been to second base with your boyfriend, right?"

Her question caught me off guard and made me uncomfortable. So I didn't answer. Dawn's grin turned into a puzzled stare. "No way! What about first base?"

Dawn started giggling. "I guess by your silence we can say that's a definite N-O."

The other two girls joined in the laughter. But Sabrina said nothing.

"You know what?" Dawn sneered. "I bet you don't even have a boyfriend and probably never had one." The smug look on Dawn's round face and her teasing made my blood boil.

And before I knew it, I blurted out, "I do have a boyfriend, and his name is Jamal."

"Oh, you mean that boy you came with?"

"Yes, we've been going together for almost two years!"

"Really, does he know about that? Because he seems to be having a great time with that girl over there."

I whipped around to see Jamal talking closely to a girl whose back was up against a wall. There were other couples doing the same thing—some were even kissing.

My cheeks flaming, I shot up and headed for a payphone. While walking away, I heard wild laughter behind me and then Sabrina said, "Why did you have to do that, Dawn?"

On the drive home, I didn't utter a word. When Cynthia asked me what was wrong, I couldn't answer her question. And when Jamal asked me the same thing, he got nothing from me either.

Why did he have to do that? I seethed inside.

Even though I had no reason to be mad at Jamal, I just was—just like I was angry with myself for not being like a normal teenager. Why wasn't I into fashion or fixing my hair? And why wasn't Jamal my boyfriend?

Chapter 25

LATER that night, I found myself critiquing my body in the hanging mirror behind my bedroom door. I had breasts. I had a shapely pear figure. And from what I'd been told, I had a pretty face. So I couldn't understand why Jamal was attracted to that girl at the skating rink more than me. That was just *one* of two things still bothering me. The other had to do with looking like a fool. I couldn't believe I told that lie and got busted on it—right in front of those cackling girls. *Oh, the humiliation!*

Eager to sleep the day away, I tied my hair up with a silk scarf and then slipped under the covers. And just when I felt myself drifting into oblivion, I heard tapping at my window.

"Are you kidding me?" I murmured, getting out of bed.

I lifted the window and gave Jamal a stern look. "It's eleven o'clock at night. What could you possibly want at this hour?"

"Let me in," he whispered.

"Are you crazy? I can't pull your tall behind through this window without waking up my parents. Look, just go to the front porch, and I'll meet you there."

I put on my shorts, my tennis shoes, and a light jacket and then tiptoed toward the front door. When I eased my way out,

I turned off the porch light. The new streetlight at the end of the driveway was bright enough.

"You haven't knocked on my window in over a year, so what's going on?" I asked, sitting down next to Jamal on the steps.

"I just wanted to make sure you're okay. You seemed pretty vexed back at the skating rink."

"It was nothing, Jamal. I'm over it now."

"Well, are you going to tell me about it?"

"No, that's not necessary. I just want to forget the whole thing."

"Lovely," Jamal said, taking on a rare serious tone, "I'm not leaving until you tell me what happened."

Obviously, he wasn't going to take no for an answer. So I decided to tell him about Dawn but skip what I saw him doing.

"I kind of got into it with Sabrina's friend, Dawn. She started teasing me about not having a boyfriend and not letting a boy feel me up. She just really got under my skin; that's why I wanted to come home early."

Jamal sucked his teeth. "That's it? That's what got you so upset? Look, I saw that skeezer and she was not cute. Trust me, the only reason she has a boyfriend is because she's giving it up easily. You don't have to do that to get a guy."

"Really, you think I could get a boyfriend?"

"Yes!" he said with certainty. "Why couldn't you? You're smart, pretty and you have a huge heart. How many other kids you know take care of their parents the way you do?"

Jamal put his arms around me and I began to feel that warm sensation again.

"So, you think I'm pretty?" I asked, leaning on his shoulder with a grin.

"Of course I do! I mean, if you weren't like a sister to me, I would of asked you to be my girl a long time ago."

"A sister," I repeated, pulling away and deflating like a balloon.

"Yeah, you're my sister." He nudged me with his elbow. "My road-dog."

And there it was. For the second time, Jamal reminded me that he would only see me as a friend—never as a girlfriend. In that moment, I let go of the thought of Jamal being my first real boyfriend.

"So why don't *you* have a girl yet?" I asked, trying to mask my disappointment. "Or maybe you do and you just haven't told me about her."

"Nah, you know I tell you everything. Besides, I'm not claiming anybody. I rather play the field."

"You dog." I chuckled.

"Roof, roof," he joked. "Hey, who's that creeping into your aunt's driveway with their headlights off?"

I turned my head and focused in.

"Not sure. Maybe that's Cynthia with her boyfriend," I said.

"Rolling in an old station wagon like that?" He shook his head. "Nah, I don't think so."

"Well, I know his name is Greg, but I don't know what kind of car he drives. I just hope Cynthia doesn't get caught coming in so late."

"What do you mean—get caught? Isn't she grown?"

"Oh, yeah...try telling Aunt Harriet that."

Jamal laughed.

"No, wait—look," I said. "That's Uncle Nathan coming out of the house. Chucky is his only friend and that's not him. So, who's in the car?"

"Yo! That reminds me," Jamal said urgently. "I forget to tell you something."

"Tell me what?" He piqued my interest.

"About two weeks ago, my mom saw your uncle at a corner store over in Stanton Manor, you know—the hood. Well, she said she saw him in the parking lot talking to a known drug dealer who goes by the name Peaches."

"So what are you trying say?" I asked, shooting him a disapproving look. "My uncle is on drugs and that's a drug dealer over there making a midnight house call? By the way, why was your mother in the hood?"

"Hey, chill out with that!" He waved me off. "My cousin lives in Stanton and my mom went there to get her hair braided. Lovely, you of all people should know my mom wouldn't tell me something like that if it wasn't true."

I nodded. "Yeah, you're right...sorry for being defensive."

"It's all right." He patted my back. "Maybe it's nothing. Maybe that's just a friend over there y'all know nothing about."

Jamal stood up to stretch and yawn. "Hey, I'm about to go home. Are you good?"

I flashed a smile.

"Great, now go to bed and forget about that girl."

Jamal walked off into the night.

Chapter 26

LYING on a blanket in the field, I lazily watched clouds float by and take on different shapes and forms. I saw a duck, a man riding an elephant, the profile of a gorilla and I swear, Mrs. Hanes—my overweight home economics teacher from sixth grade. But my favorite type of cloud was the one that resembled a giant bowl of whipped cream. Oh, how I loved those. When I was younger, I used to imagine myself jumping from bowl to bowl—eating my way happily through the sky.

It was the middle of June and yet the gentle, steady breeze made the afternoon heat bearable for a picnic and a good read underneath an umbrella. This time, my book of choice was *The Lord of the Rings*—an epic tale about little people, elves, and a wizard on a quest to destroy an evil, magical ring in a faraway land. A perfect book to read among a backdrop of chirping birds and rustling tree leaves to send my imagination soaring.

Last week I began doing things differently to change up my daily routine and get my mind off my boring life, starting with reading outdoors instead of in my bedroom and venturing into fantasy novels instead of the mystery crime books I usually read. Keeping up with my appearance was something else I vowed to do.

Ever since that embarrassing incident back at the skating rink, I'd kept to myself—only speaking to Sabrina when she called to apologize for Dawn's rudeness. Of course I accepted. But, I'd also come to accept the fact that I may not be like most teenage girls. So what if I didn't have a boyfriend yet? So what I hadn't been to second base and still had my virginity? "All things in due time" is what Mama would say. And at the age of thirteen and a half, I was cool with that.

I picked up my book again to finish the last twenty or so pages when I heard fussing break out.

"You came back here almost two o'clock in the morning. I'm tired of you disrespecting me and my rules," I heard Aunt Harriet say when I got closer to the window on the side of the house. "And now you're leaving out here with a big overnight bag. I—"

"Mama, I'm just going out with Greg after work," Cynthia interrupted.

"What kind of unmarried, young girl goes to a man's house to just change clothes? There's nothing new under the sun. You're sleeping with him, aren't you?"

"Yes, yes!" Cynthia shouted. "We're having sex. So what! I'm not a little girl anymore, Mama. And it's 1987—nobody waits for marriage anymore either."

"Well, since you're grown enough to lay up with a man, then you're grown enough to take care of yourself, missy, because I don't take care of grown people."

"Are you kidding me? Then what about Uncle Nathan? He doesn't work! He doesn't contribute to the house! And he comes and goes as he pleases—you take of care of him."

"Listen to your nasty mouth. *Lord*, where did I go wrong with this child?"

A car horn honked.

"Where are you going? I'm still talking to you!" Aunt Harriet hollered.

"Away. And I'm not coming back. Just think of me as one less grown person you have to take care of."

When I heard the screen door slam, I ran up the side of the house to get a peek from the porch. And as the blue Firebird pulled away, I could see Cynthia hunched over crying.

Chapter 27

"WHERE did I go wrong, Dolores?" Aunt Harriet said, sitting at the kitchen table stirring a cup of hot tea. "You raise these babies up from the crib only to see them turn against you in the end." Mama placed a hand on Aunt Harriet's shoulder as she set a saucer of bread pudding in front of her. "You still haven't heard from her?" she asked, taking a seat.

"No," Aunt Harriet answered.

"Well, it's only eight o'clock. Let's just see if she comes home tonight."

Mama sipped the tea then shook her head. "You haven't done anything wrong, Harriet. I just think that man has Miss Cynthia feeling grown and now she wants to test her wings. This too shall pass."

"Well, as far as I'm concerned, Miss Cynthia can keep her tail where she's at. You know, Dolores, sometimes I think I got the wrong one."

"What do you mean by that?" Mama asked.

"I mean, I should have gotten Lovely."

I stopped washing dishes and looked back again, thinking I didn't want to be pulled into this drama. Aunt Harriet was upset. So I dared not to say a word and just kept listening in.

"Lovely is respectful," Aunt Harriet continued. "She does what she's told plus she helps out around the house. You've never had any problems with her. But me and Cynthia—all we do is lock horns."

"C'mon, Harriet, you don't mean that. You're just upset right now."

"Sheeet, the hell I do!" Aunt Harriet hissed. "You should of heard the way that child spoke to me today. So much disrespect...so much filth. If I had the strength, I would of slapped the taste out her mouth."

"Now, I have to admit, Cynthia can get a little feisty at times. But, so were you at that age. If you think about it, Harriet, you and Cynthia are more alike than you think." Mama chuckled. "Maybe that's why you two keep getting into these spats. Y'all can't communicate because you're too busy trying to tell each other off."

"That may be the case, but I didn't talk to our parents like that. These kids are different today. They've got no manners; they're sleeping around and wearing all these tight clothes. But, what bothers me the most—beyond her tone of voice and words—is the fact she didn't think of me enough, as her mother, to introduce me to her boyfriend. A twenty-four-year-old man she's been dating for the last month who has his own apartment. For all I know, he could be a lunatic and strangle the life out of her. Then what would I tell the police? 'Sorry officers, I can't give you a description of the man because I never met him.'"

Aunt Harriet paused. It sounded like she was becoming emotional, which was rare.

"Dolores, we just didn't do things like this in our day. You brought the gentleman home so everybody can get a look at him. That was the proper way."

"I know, Harriet. Times have definitely changed; trust me, I've noticed."

Then suddenly, Mama called out. "Harriet, are you okay? You look flushed."

I turned around. Aunt Harriet had her fingers on her wrist, like she was feeling her pulse.

"I think my blood pressure is up," she said. "My nerves were so bad today I forgot to take my medicine."

"I guess so," Mama said. "Harriet, you've got to calm down. Just sit here and relax." Mama looked at me. "Lovely, go on over to Harriet's house and get her blood pressure medicine for me, please."

"It's in the blue and white bottle on my dresser," Aunt Harriet said.

"Yes, ma'am." I dried my hands then left the kitchen.

***

Aunt Harriet's bedroom smelled like Bengay. Her bottle of blood pressure pills was exactly where she said it would be. I switched off the light and then closed the door. That's when I heard loud—almost dangerous sounding—snoring down the hall. I knew I needed to get back to Aunt Harriet, pronto, but those sounds piqued my interest. I walked up to Uncle Nathan's door and slowly pushed my way in to get a quick peek. Those noises now sounded like gurgling.

"Uncle Nathan," I said as I turned the light on.

He didn't respond. I came in a little closer to make sure he was all right. And that's when I saw things on Uncle Nathan I should have never seen. He was lying on his back topless with some type of rubber tie around his left arm. There was a needle on the floor. And most shocking, his penis was hanging out of his shorts.

I felt myself change in an instant. My heart started pumping fast and I couldn't look away. I had never seen a real penis before—not even my dad's. I remembered diagrams of penises in a sex education class, but nothing like this. Uncle Nathan's penis was wide and flopped over. I don't why I did it, maybe curiosity got the best of me, but I stretched out my finger and nervously poked it.

Yuck—sticky!

"It's okay. You can touch it," Uncle Nathan said as he grabbed my hand and placed it on his penis. "You're just curious, that's all."

"No!" I gasped, throwing my left hand over my mouth. I never noticed he stopped snoring. "I didn't mean to," I said, trying to pull away.

"Shh. Shh. It's okay. This will be our little secret. I won't tell anyone you wanted to touch my dick." He began stroking my hand on it rapidly.

"No," I continued to cry out and break free from his strong grip.

Then suddenly, the phone rang.

And that's when Uncle Nathan finally let go and I ran out fast.

"I'm sorry, Lovely. I'm not well. Please forgive me!" I heard him yell.

I stood on the porch and dried my eyes before going back into the house. And I kept my head low when I put the medicine on the kitchen table.

"I just called over there. What took you so long?" Mama asked.

Walking away toward the bathroom, I answered, "I couldn't find the bottle."

Chapter 28

IN one of my trembling hands I held a cookie and in the other, a tall glass of milk. I was sitting in my room alone with the door locked dealing with my emotions in silence. I just discovered eating almost an entire bag of Chips Ahoy! was the only thing I could do soothe my soul and stop me from crying.

The coldness of the glass stung my hand. Both of my palms were still red and sore, even an hour later, from all the scrubbing I did—trying to clean away the sensation of Uncle Nathan's nasty dick off my palms.

I snickered inside, acknowledging my hypocrisy. I called him nasty. But I was nasty too!

I was nasty for touching him first and feeling excited when I did. So how could I report his crime when I was just as guilty?

I felt an enormous embarrassment and shame. There was no way I would tell anyone. Not even Jamal. And to think, Cynthia and Jamal had it right the whole time. Not only was Uncle Nathan a sick pervert...he was also a drug addict.

A long time ago, I heard someone say, "What goes on in the dark must shine someday in the light." In this case, I prayed that would truly happen. Because Uncle Nathan would have to get exposed for who he really was without me having to go to the police.

Leaning over to put the glass of milk on the nightstand, I caught a glimpse of my face in a mirror. I looked worn out, like I had aged five years. And my eyes were red and swollen. I wondered if Uncle Nathan saw me now, looking like an old hag, would he call me pretty? Would he still find me just as attractive as Corinne?

As I pondered those questions, grief started to bubble up inside me again. It traveled from my stomach up into my chest—trying hard to fight its way out. I got so tired of crying. My eyes stung and my throat was already sore. But the overwhelming pain made me give in.

Sliding underneath the sheets with my grief, I hugged a pillow thinking how I no longer cared about being pretty. Pretty only got me unwanted attention from a dirty old man. So I sobbed into that pillow making a pledge: *From this point on, I'll make sure to look like shit. That way, no man will ever want me.*

Chapter 29

SITTING in the lobby, the receptionist's big, blonde hair captured my attention. I wondered how long it took her to tease it this morning and how much Aqua Net hairspray was used to get it to stand up so high. My guesses were two hours and the entire can. This new trend sweeping the country looked ridiculous—just like those slimy Jheri curls I thought would have gone out of style by now but kept popping up like weeds.

I laughed inside and scratched my matted scalp.

Okay. I absolutely had no right to judge somebody else's hair, especially, when mine was such a hot mess. I stopped taking care of it a long time ago, so the roots were dry and frizzy and hadn't been touched by a straightening comb in weeks. These days I did the bare minimum—a quick brushed-back ponytail—and that was all. A few times, Mama raised concerns and offered to press my hair. But I declined, of course, to stay true to my vows. I didn't give a hoot about my looks. Just like I didn't care about wearing this wrinkled pink, blue and yellow tie-dye T-shirt today, which I had been recycling all week without washing it.

I was waiting on Mama to come out of the doctor's office at any minute. She'd been in there for almost an hour to get Daddy's test results. About a week ago, Daddy started complaining of a slight pain when urinating. At first, Mama thought it was just a small stone that would pass. But when she noticed blood in his urine, she got him an appointment for lab work right away.

The light wooden door swung open and Mama finally came out. She looked serious—way too serious. And that told me something was very wrong. I stood up.

"Mama, is everything okay?"

She gave me a dazed looked and then said, "Here, take your father's arm and go ahead to the car. I've got to check out."

***

Mama got into the car with a distant facial expression. Without a word, she fastened her seatbelt, started up the engine, placed her hands on the steering wheel, and looked straight ahead. I don't even think she blinked.

Her silence made me nervous. "Mama, is everything okay?" I asked again.

Mama took a glance at Daddy sleeping in the passenger's seat. Then she looked at me from the rearview mirror. "No." She shook her head. "Everything is not okay."

She began to sniffle and that's when I scooted up beside her and saw a tear rolling down her cheek. "Mama, what's wrong? Please tell me what's wrong."

Mama pulled out some tissue and wiped her face. Speaking in a stronger voice she said, "Your father is very sick. He has prostate cancer."

"What? What do you mean? They can fix him, right?"

Mama shook her head. "No. He's already in the third stage. There's not much they can do for him now—except make him comfortable with pain medications."

"So he's dying!" I cried.

"Yes." She nodded. "They've given him less than a year."

"No Daddy, no!" I moaned, sliding back into my seat. Slumped over with my arms covering my face, I heard Mama say, "Now listen to me, Lovely. We've got to be strong for your father. You know he wouldn't want us to worry like this. So whatever time left the good Lord has for him on this earth, we've just got to make the best of it."

Mama put the car in gear. "Yes, that's what we must do," she said then drove off.

I heard Mama's words of wisdom but I thought it was all unfair. And I was beginning to question just how good God really was. He'd already taken Irene from us and now he wanted Daddy too. I didn't know where I'd find the strength to deal with another death as well as the recent incident with Uncle Nathan. All the way home, I kept pondering...

Why would a good God let so many bad things happen all at once?

Chapter 30

"MARK my words!" Ms. Lorraine declared. "That Oprah Winfrey show is going to beat Donahue's show in the ratings...it's just a matter of time."

"What are you talking about, girl? *The Phil Donahue Show* has been around for decades. He's not going anywhere," Mama countered.

"Well, I didn't say the man was going somewhere. I'm just saying there's a new sheriff in town. Do you know how much those white folks love Oprah Winfrey?"

Addie chuckled. "She's gotta point there, Mama. You should see her studio audience—just a room full of them."

"Yep," "Sure enough," "That's right," "Mhmm," people around the table agreed.

"Well, I think the woman's smart and a good talker," Lorraine continued. "You can tell she's gonna be around for a long time because she's got that...whatcha call it?" She started snapping her fingers.

"Staying power," Aunt Harriet said.

"Yeah, that." Ms. Lorraine pointed.

Sunday, August 9. We were having a dinner party to celebrate Daddy's life. Mama said we should give flowers to love ones while they're alive not just when they're dead. One by one, Mama had close friends and family members stand up and say something to Daddy. It was like that old television show I'd seen reruns of, *This is Your Life*. While some of the comments were emotional, most of them were lighthearted and downright funny. I think for most people, especially Mama, grieving for Daddy started the moment he was diagnosed with Parkinson's disease several years ago, which made the recent news of his terminal health expected—but no less hurtful in my opinion.

The turnout was good, about thirty people or so. I cooked most of the food while Mama took care of Daddy's needs. Even sitting at the table, I never took my apron off—as a hostess I was always on duty. I grabbed another yeast roll. It was my third. Aunt Harriet, sitting next to me, noticed. "Remember…a moment on your lips, a lifetime on your hips," she teased in a whisper. That was the second time today somebody made a sly remark about my weight gain or appearance. Earlier today Deidra told me all I needed was a head scarf and I'd look just like Aunt Jemima with my apron and round, pudgy face. I responded with a death stare and a balled fist. That was one good thing about gaining weight: Deidra knew I could knock her out flat.

Rolling my eyes, I paid no attention to Aunt Harriet and went on to butter my bread when I heard, "Hey, hey! How's everybody doing tonight?"

It was Uncle Nathan standing right next to me. Instantly, the blood in my veins went cold and I became paralyzed like a deer in the headlights. For two months, we'd been able to avoid each other. He stopped eating dinner with us while I did everything to evade going into Aunt Harriet's house. And now the sound of his creepy voice was within earshot and making me sick to my stomach.

I dropped my bread and managed to slide over in my chair without making a scene.

"Hi Nathan," Mama said warmly. "Pull up a chair. I'm glad to see you decided to stop by. I heard you weren't feeling well earlier."

"Oh, I'm better now," he said, pushing a chair in between Aunt Harriet and me. "I got nothing to complain about. Besides, I wouldn't miss this for anything in the world. How you doing, Mr. Joseph?"

I scoffed at Uncle Nathan's comment. I bet he felt better because he just got high.

"Good, good," Mama responded.

"Hey, Harriet," Uncle Nathan spoke low, "did you notice the rest of Cynthia's stuff is gone? She came by this morning with her boyfriend."

"Yeah, I noticed. It's a damn shame she waited until I went to church so she wouldn't have to face me. That child didn't even have the decency to say goodbye to her own mother."

"Well, don't you go worrying yourself about Cynthia," he said. "I guarantee she'll return when she finds out just how cold the world can be."

Uncle Nathan started chuckling then switched his attention to me. "And how are you doing, Miss Lovely?"

That was it! The moment he uttered my name, I shot up out of my seat like a rocket on blast.

Heads turned.

"What's wrong with you?" Aunt Harriet asked.

"Yes, Lovely, where are you going so fast?" Mama asked, giving me a curious squint.

"To the bathroom," I answered. "Excuse me."

I stormed past the bathroom, went into my bedroom, and locked the door. With nostrils flaring, I angrily paced the floor until I felt a strong urge to crawl underneath the bed and grab my secret stash of goodies. I tore open the box of Debbie Cakes. They couldn't get in my mouth fast enough.

How dare that bastard have the audacity to call out my name!

Chapter 31

I sat behind the bus driver where I felt most comfortable. The seats at the front were typically reserved for the nerds and outcasts who wanted to avoid being teased by the kids at the back of the bus. It was Friday, August 28, 1987 and I had just gotten through my second week as a freshman at Willisburg High School. I'd always believed the first couple of weeks of school determine so much: your classes, the relationships you'll have with teachers, and what your status would be among peers and friends. For me, I already knew my college prep courses were going to be a challenge and I'd get along with my teachers. But I also knew my friendship with Sabrina had faded away.

Sabrina and I didn't share any classes this year. And we barely spoke in full sentences the few times we saw each other in the hallways. "Hi," she would say to me in passing and I'd politely reply in the same way. But I suspected that would soon end as well.

Sabrina didn't do a thing to me. I stopped talking to her because we lived in two different worlds now. Her world consisted of plenty of friends and hangouts at the mall. My world dealt with chores and isolation. I looked up to Sabrina in the past, but when I lost interest in my appearance, I stopped seeing her as a fashion icon or a source of inspiration. And I definitely didn't care about being in the loop of all things teenager anymore.

Luckily, Jamal and I were still close. But even though we talked every day and had English class together, he no longer sat next to me on the bus. He now sat with a group of boys at the back, clowning around and talking. Usually, the bus would be filled with Jamal's loud laughter. But he and his band mates stayed after school to get ready for tonight's annual Sertoma Football game.

The moment I got into the house, I headed for one of my housecoats to change. Then I knocked on my parents' bedroom door. "Mama, I'm home. Do you need anything?"

"Come on in," she said.

I pushed the door open to find Mama sitting on the side of the bed with a bucket to Daddy's face. He was throwing up again.

"Is he still having trouble keeping food down?"

"Yeah." Mama nodded. "But he only threw up once today. He held down his breakfast good, so that's a blessing." She smiled. "So how was school today?"

"It was good. I'm really enjoying my classes."

"That's nice. I'm glad to hear that. Are you going to the Sertoma with Sabrina tonight?"

"No ma'am," I answered. "I thought I'd just hang out here and help you out."

Mama wiped Daddy's mouth. "Are you done, Joseph?" she asked loudly. Daddy nodded and then Mama began to straighten him up and adjust his pillows.

"You know, Lovely, I'm sure we can manage without you. You should go out and enjoy yourself." She gave me a backward glance. Then she started laughing.

"What's so funny?" I asked.

"Oh, I was just remembering how Irene used to love going to those Sertoma games. She said they set the tone for the football season and the beginning of the school year. And she just loved to watch those marching bands get down on the field." Mama shook her head. "Oh, I miss my baby girl." She pulled the green comforter up to Daddy's chest. "Are you comfortable, Joseph?" she shouted. Daddy blinked his eyes and nodded.

"Good," she said, leaning over to kiss his cheek. "You sleep tight."

Mama turned her attention to me. "Lovely, I want you to go to that Sertoma tonight. You do a lot around here. Now it's time for you to have some fun."

I smiled halfheartedly, knowing she was right. But these days I just preferred to stay to myself and avoid crowds. "Maybe next year, Mama."

Mama seemed bothered by my response.

"Lovely, I know I've been busy with your father lately. But I've been meaning to talk with you for months. I'm concerned about you. You're so much different nowadays. You isolate yourself in your room, you're not keeping up with your hair anymore, Sabrina doesn't call, and honey...you've put on some weight."

I dropped my face.

"Now, hold on, I want you to look at me. I'm not picking on you. You will always be my beautiful baby girl—no matter the size. But is there something bothering you? Is there something you want to talk to me about?"

Mama set up the perfect moment for me to tell my secret. I took a glimpse at Daddy's sickly pale face. He was gazing up at the ceiling, disconnected. And yet I still couldn't tell her about my deep-seated shame.

I forced a fake grin. "Really, Mama, I'm fine. I guess I've just been stressed out about going into high school and eating too many cookies in the process. So, please, don't worry about me."

Mama narrowed her eyes as though she wasn't totally convinced.

"Okay, if you say so. But do this much for me so I can worry less…slow down on those cookies and find some time to have fun and live your life." She cupped my face with her hands. "You're young, child…so be young. And don't be concerning yourself about high school either. You're sharp as a tack, and you know this."

There was no place to hide looking into Mama's eyes. It took everything in me to hold back the truth and my tears. "Yes, ma'am," I said. "I promise to try."

Chapter 32

FOR Mama's sake, I found the willpower to get up early Monday morning to fix my hair and put on ironed clothes before going to school. It was my attempt to keep my promise to do better and look like somebody instead of a ragamuffin.

I closed my locker door only to find Jamal staring back at me with a smirk on his face and his trumpet case at his feet. "You're looking good today. I haven't seen you this cleaned up in a long time. So what's the occasion?"

"No occasion." I shrugged. "Just felt like doing something different."

"Well, your hair looks nice." He bobbed his head in approval. "I've missed your hair looking nice."

I flashed a smile. "Thanks. By the way, why weren't you on the bus this morning?"

"Oh, I overslept and missed the bus. My mom's boyfriend gave me a ride to school on his way to work."

"Wow, Mr. Gerald is really hanging in there. He and your mom have been together almost a year, right?"

"Yep, he's not bad. Better than the others. At least he can keep a job."

"You know what I'm thinking, right? Soon, you'll be calling him dad…officially."

Jamal chuckled. "I don't know about that. It hasn't been a whole year yet, we'll see."

The bell rang, signaling us to go for second period.

"Hey, I've got algebra class. I'll talk to you later."

***

I walked into class just in time to beat the late bell and took a seat at the back of the room. I tried to get comfortable, but I hated those one-size-fits-all chair and desk combos at Willisburg High School. The small, square-shaped seats were hard and would often put my butt to sleep. Many times I had to rock side to side just to get my blood circulating again. I think the designers must've had stick figures in mind instead of growing teenagers with hips, thighs, and backsides while drawing up the diagram.

I enjoyed Algebra almost as much as I enjoyed reading. Like a good mystery book, I loved solving x, y, and z if the equation required it. To me, reading and math problems were similar in the way they made me feel: they helped me focus and block out the world. But I didn't do much talking in class even when I knew the answer to a problem on the board. Like in all of my classes, I preferred to do just the three L's: listen, look, and learn.

Mrs. O'Reilly, the teacher, asked us to swap our take home quiz she assigned last Friday to the person next to us for grading. According to the paper, I swapped with a boy named Patrick Helmsley. It was only the third week of school so I didn't know much about him or anyone else in the class. But I noticed Patrick had a friendly smile.

The lights were dimmed and then answers to the quiz popped up on a white screen powered by an overhead projector. Low moans and groans echoed throughout the room.

"By your sounds, I guess I shouldn't expect excellent grades from you guys," Mrs. O'Reilly said. "Well, no worries. You'll get this. I'll take it step-by-step."

Mrs. O'Reilly broke down every equation to its simplest form. I understood the lesson, but a few students were still sighing in confusion, including Patrick.

The projector went off and the room became bright again.

"Okay, students. Swap the papers back to their owners. When you're done looking over your quizzes, pass them up. In the meantime, I'm handing out tonight's homework. And remember, people…along with understanding the basics, showing your work is the key to mastering algebra."

"You got every question right—even the bonus," Patrick said, wide-eyed.

I handed Patrick his quiz. He got a 60. "Sorry I can't say the same to you."

"Ah, it's okay." He shrugged. "I've never been good in math anyway."

I had no idea what to say except, "Practice makes perfect."

"I guess so," he said.

The school bell rung for the next period.

"Hey, guys, listen up before you leave!" Mrs. O'Reilly shouted. "You know we're having our first test next week. So, if any of you feel you don't have a handle on this stuff, come see me now."

While leaving class, I looked back and saw Patrick talking to the teacher. He looked stressed out. For his sake, I hope he'd get help before the test.

Chapter 33

THE cafeteria buzzed with activity. The sounds of people talking, clinking pots, pans, and trays along with outbursts of obnoxious laughter engulfed the room. A quick scan showed that students were now settled into their respective groups. That would be your jocks, the popular, the band-heads, the nerds, the loners, and finally—the weird.

I walked a fine line between the loners and the bookworms. For the second week in a row, I'd been sitting among a few members of the book club I joined last week during lunch. I sat here not so much for conversation or friendship. In fact, we barely said anything to each other. The only time we had an exciting exchange was when someone brought up V.C. Andrew's controversial novel, *Flowers in the Attic*. Truth be told, I had no idea where I fit in. So I'd been sitting there, at the end of the table, hiding, knowing I wouldn't get any judgment or expectations from these bookworms. But Mama was right. I had changed and become more withdrawn. Things I found interest in were no longer appealing, like searching for Corinne. But thank God I still loved my books.

I raised my chocolate milk to my mouth to suddenly see Patrick Helmsley looking down at me. "Can I sit?" he asked.

I wiped my mouth. "Sure," I replied, wondering what in the world he could want.

"So, you really impressed me with your math skills this morning."

"Thanks." I smiled.

"Listen, you really seem to understand this algebra stuff very well and obviously, I don't. So, what do you think about helping me out? You know, tutoring me after school? I talked to Mrs. O'Reilly about you and she agreed—you'd be the perfect person to study with."

Just as Patrick was asking me for help, I looked over his shoulder and saw Jamal staring back at me from across the cafeteria. He was sitting with Quincy McNeil and some other boys.

"Lovely, I really need to pass this test next week. So what do you say? Can you tutor me?"

I shifted my eyes from Jamal to Patrick. And with a wide grin I answered, "Sure, when do you want to start?"

"As soon as possible."

***

I got off the school bus thinking about today's unexpected events.

"Wait up, girl. Why are you rushing?" I heard behind me.

I stopped.

"What are you talking about, Jamal? I'm walking at my normal pace."

"Okay, if you say so. I just thought you was trying to get home fast to talk to your new friend on the phone."

"What new friend?" I asked, playing dumb. I knew exactly who he was referring to.

"You know who I'm talking about. I'm talking about that big-head boy you were talking to during lunch."

I chuckled. "Oh, stop it. You know Patrick does not have a big head."

"So that's his name—Patrick."

"Yes, Patrick Hemsley. You don't know him?"

"No. Am I supposed to?"

"Well, no. I just thought because you're such a social butterfly now, you may know something about him. But I guess not." I shrugged then began walking again.

"So are you going to tell me what you two were talking about?"

I laughed. "You know, Jamal, it almost sounds like you're jealous. Are you jealous?"

He sucked his teeth. "Hell, no! You know better than that. I'm just watching out for my home-girl."

"Well, if you have to know, Patrick asked me to tutor him in algebra, that's all."

"That's all," Jamal said, rolling his eyes. "I don't think so. I got a look at the smile on his face when he walked away from your table...I think he's into you."

"He's into me...no way." I shook my head.

"Why not?" Jamal asked in a serious voice.

I stopped walking again. The thought of revealing my true feelings made me cringe. But it was Jamal and I could share this with him.

"I do think Patrick is handsome. But…" I trailed off.

"But what? Spit it out."

"I don't think I'm his type, okay. I've gained a lot of weight this year, and he just seems like the type that would be attracted to skinny girls."

"You don't know that. Besides, even with the weight gain, you're still pretty, especially when you fix yourself up."

"Thank you."

"You're welcome, but you really should have more confidence in yourself. Whatever happened to that brave girl who used to pick up snakes and climb tall trees?"

"Ha. I was a tomboy, wasn't I?"

"Yes, you were. Listen, why don't you use this opportunity to get to know Patrick a little better? You know…feel him out. And if things are good, ask him out to the movies. Didn't you say you wanted to see *Masters of the Universe?*"

"Oh, I can't do that, Jamal."

"Sure you can. When do you start tutoring him?"

"Tomorrow at lunch, but he's coming over to my house on Saturday."

"Perfect!" Jamal said, delighted. "Now you can start buttering him up for the kill. And please, please, please…do keep your hair done because that nappy mess you had going on this past summer was not cute at all."

I started laughing. "Shut up." I tried swatting his arm. I missed. He moved too fast.

"Ha. You've got to be quicker than that," he teased.

I started chasing Jamal down the road. "If I were in better shape, I'd catch you and give you a good beating," I hollered.

"I know—that's why I'm making you run," he yelled back. "You wanted to lose weight, right?" Before I knew it, Jamal's neon green shirt became a speck in the distance.

I never did catch that rabbit.

Chapter 34

NESTLED in Daddy's old recliner in the den, I was watching an old episode of *What's Happening!* when I heard loud knocking at the front door. I looked at the clock above the television—11:23 PM. I furrowed my brows. "Who is that this time of night?"

When I reached the door, I peered through the peephole then opened it.

"Aunt Harriet, you look upset. Is everything all right?"

"Girl, where's your mother?" she asked, walking in.

"I'm right here," Mama said, tying her robe. "What's wrong, Harriet?"

"Your brother! That's what's wrong!" she said, breathing hard.

Mama took on a frightened gaze. "What do you mean? What's wrong with Nathan?"

"Oh, he ain't dead, Dolores," she said, sitting down on the couch. "But I'd like to kill him."

"Harriet, you're not making any sense. What's happened to Nathan?"

"I'll tell ya what's happened. Our brother is on drugs and has got himself caught up with a thug drug dealer."

"What! Where are you getting all this from?"

"It all started earlier today when some man named Peaches called the house looking for Nathan."

My eyes grew big the instant I heard that name—that was the drug dealer Jamal spoke of back in June.

"I told him he wasn't home," Aunt Harriet continued, "and that's when Peaches told me Nathan owed him money for a package and he would be coming by to collect for it soon."

Mama and I sat down to hear the rest of Aunt Harriet's story.

"Naturally, I asked what kind of package did Nathan buy from him and how much did it cost? The man told me it was medicine and Nathan owed twenty-five dollars."

"Twenty-five dollars?! What kind of medicine costs twenty-five dollars?" Mama asked.

Crack! I rejoiced in my head. Uncle Nathan just got busted.

"I'm getting to that, Dolores." Aunt Harriet picked up a magazine from the coffee table and began fanning herself with it. "When I got off the phone, I went through Nathan's dresser drawers and found needles. You know—the kind you get from the doctor's office."

"You mean syringes, Aunt Harriet?"

"Yes, those."

"Nathan isn't a diabetic," Mama pointed out. "So what's he doing with syringes?"

"And that's what I wanted to know too. Oh, I couldn't wait until Mr. Nathan got his tail home, because I had a lot of questions that needed answering. And don't you know the moment Chucky dropped Nathan off, that Peaches boy pulled up right behind them? It was like he was watching my house the entire night…makes my nerves bad just thinking about it."

"So, what did Peaches do?" I asked.

"He demanded his money, of course. But Nathan didn't have it. And that's when Peaches threatened to kick his behind. So guess who had to pay him off?" Aunt Harriet slapped her thigh with the magazine. "*Me!*"

"My Lord," Mama said.

"Dolores, our baby brother is a heroin addict. He's been shooting up heroin for years trying to relieve his so-called back pain…at least that's how he explained it."

"Heroin." Mama groaned, pressing a hand against her chest. She looked more disappointed than shocked—like she knew he was capable of using something so harsh.

"Yeah, but I don't buy that back pain story," Aunt Harriet said, shaking her head. "We've been through this before…remember, Dolores? Remember when that boy used to suck down liquor like a fish and piss on himself? Sheeet…what a fool I was to think he'd come back here a changed man. I'm telling you—Nathan is still fighting demons only God can help him battle. He really does need some help. He needs to get himself in a good church."

When did all this happen, Aunt Harriet?"

"About forty minutes ago."

"So where's Nathan right now?" Mama asked, sounding exhausted.

"I don't know, Dolores. After I paid that money, I told Nathan to get out of my house and never come back until he's completely clean. I don't need this type of stress and aggravation at my age. Don't you know—that man could of killed us tonight!"

"You're right, Harriet. That drug dealer could have done anything to y'all. That's why we should call the police."

"Oh, no, don't do that!" Aunt Harriet said sharply. "The last thing we need is trouble from a drug dealer. He's gone. Nathan's gone. Let's just put this whole thing behind us."

Another twenty minutes went by until Aunt Harriet stopped venting, and still, her nerves were so unsettled she decided to spend the night. I had never seen her rattled before—too frightened to sleep in her own bed. When I returned to my bedroom, I turned off the light, pulled back the curtains, and stared across the street. Aunt Harriet's house was dark with no signs of movement. It was true—Uncle Nathan was really gone. Finally, God answered one of my prayers. And for the first time in many nights, I went to bed without knots in my stomach.

Chapter 35

I got up the next morning feeling rested—like I had just awoken from a month-long hibernation. My mind was clear. My body felt energized. And my mood was light. Just in time for my afternoon study date with Patrick Hemsley.

I took Jamal's advice. During the week, I got the chance to learn a little more about Patrick. I learned he was into baseball, enjoyed reading like me, and his father was the reason he sought help in algebra. According to Patrick, Mr. Hemsley expected him to get good grades and go to college just like he did. But, most importantly, I discovered that Patrick wasn't a dummy. After learning how to organize his work, he started see how structured and easy algebra could be, which made teaching him satisfying.

I heard a car pulling up into the driveway. I knew it was Patrick, so I took a final glance at myself in the mirror. "Dang it," I said, trying to pull up my stretch pants to hide my love handles. It didn't work. I could still see my fat rolls right through my X-Large shirt.

I heard a knock then I hurried off to meet him at the front door.

Patrick stood on my porch wearing a pair of black jeans and a turquoise T-shirt. He looked neat and handsome as usual. And of course, he was showing off his friendly smile.

"I'll be back in a few hours, Patrick," a woman shouted from the car.

"Is that your mom?"

"Yeah." He nodded.

"Come on in," I said, motioning with my hand.

Mama walked into the living room. "So, Lovely, this is your friend?"

"Yes ma'am, this is Patrick."

"Hello, Patrick. It's nice to meet you."

"It's nice to meet you too, Mrs. Duval."

"Now tell me something, Patrick. Do you like cake?"

"Oh, yes ma'am." He grinned.

"Good. Lovely, make sure you give Patrick a slice of the pound cake I made earlier. It should be cool by now. All right then, I'll let you kids get to your studies."

I nodded then guided Patrick to the kitchen table.

"Would you like something to drink with your cake?" I asked. "We've got milk, orange juice, tea, and red Kool-Aid."

"Sure, I'll take some Kool-Aid."

While pouring our drinks I made my mind up to ask Patrick out to the movies. He seemed cool enough. But I didn't know when would be the right time to ask. Should it be before or after our study session?

"How do you think you did on the homework?" I asked, passing him a plate of cake along with his drink.

"I actually think I did okay."

"Really?" I said, surprised. "So the fractions didn't throw you off?"

"Nope," he said with conviction.

I gave him a suspicious look and a half smirk. "Pass me your homework," I demanded. "I'll be the judge of that."

***

We went over each question, and he didn't lie. He only missed two out of twenty questions. If this were a test, he'd get a 90. What an improvement from last week.

"I told you. I told you that you'd get the hang of this!" I said, excited.

"I know." He grinned. "Now I feel confident about taking the test on Monday, which is such a relief because with my father…failure is not an option. But, of course, I've got to thank you. This wouldn't have been possible without your help."

"Aww, you're welcome," I said, blushing. "I really had fun working with you this week. I'm actually sorry it's coming to an end."

"Oh, trust me. This is not the last you'll hear from me. I'm pretty sure there'll be something else I won't understand in class, and I'll be right back at this table asking for your help."

We both started laughing; that's when I found the nerve to take a chance.

"Hey, Patrick."

"Yep."

"Do you like going to the movies?"

"Sure, I go all the time."

"Well, *Masters of the Universe* just came out. And I was wondering if you'd like to go to the movies with me to see it?"

Patrick's jovial expression faded into a serious gaze.

"You—you mean like a date?" he stuttered.

"Well…yeah."

"Lovely…" He paused. "I think you're nice and all. But I kinda got my eye on someone else at school. I'm actually planning on asking her out to the movies next weekend. Her name is Sabrina Thompson. Do you know her?"

Patrick's rejection hit me hard like a punch to the stomach. And to add salt to an open wound, he just had to mention Sabrina's name. Good ole bubbly, skinny Sabrina. In that moment, I became the best actress in the world—worthy of an Oscar *and* a Golden Globe.

"No, I don't know her," I said with the brightest, fake smile. "But I hope everything works out between the two of you."

"I hope so too. Just wish someone could introduce us. That would make things easier."

I nodded and looked at the telephone.

"Well, I think you're ready for the test. Do you need to call your mom?"

"Yeah, sure. I feel real good about algebra now. Thanks again."

"Yeah, no problem," I said politely.

For another thirty minutes, I had to tolerate Patrick until his mother came to pick him up. I wanted to scream. And I knew he must've felt a little uncomfortable too. Yet, somehow, I managed to keep up the charade and talk about random, light-hearted subjects while I stewed in my own embarrassment and humiliation. But after he left, I retreated to my bedroom with the rest of that pound cake and devoured it. *To hell with boys*, I thought. Never again would I set myself up for hurt.

Damn you, Jamal, for making me take a chance!

Chapter 36

IT was March 1988. Mama and I got the news early one morning that Cynthia had returned in the middle of the night. We hadn't heard a thing from her in almost a year, and now she was back—out of work, homeless, and with a two-month-old baby boy in her arms.

Obviously, Cynthia was already pregnant when she left home. Aunt Harriet told us over breakfast that Greg was the child's father. But the couple had been having serious problems. Last night, Cynthia found panties in Greg's car that didn't belong to her. When she confronted Greg, he admitted to cheating and told her he wasn't ready to be tied down. He wanted out. After that, Cynthia packed a bag and caught a ride home.

Aunt Harriet said the instant she saw Cynthia standing on the porch, she wanted to give her a good cussing out. There were so many nights she worried about her safety. But when she looked at that bundled-up baby and saw the hurt and desperation in Cynthia's eyes, she already knew Cynthia understood what it was like to worry about a child. So she skipped the tongue lashing and just listened.

I kept my housecoat on and put on my sneakers to go across the street. Aunt Harriet said Cynthia would bring the baby over once she had a chance to feed him and get him cleaned up. But I couldn't wait. I wanted to meet my new nephew now.

Crossing the street, I saw Cynthia sitting on the porch smoking a cigarette. Even from a short distance, I could tell she was sad.

"Hey, I heard you were back."

"Yeah, I'm back." She blew out a puff.

"When did you start smoking?" I asked.

"A few months ago," she answered then sucked in a deep drag. "It's really a filthy habit, so take my advice and don't start."

As dark gray smoke escaped her mouth, she leaned forward to smash the finished cigarette into the concrete steps next to her foot.

"I see you're still wearing those granny housecoats." She smirked.

"Yep, that's me." I shrugged. "I like to be comfortable."

Cynthia snickered and nodded her head. "I hear ya. But you know you won't catch a boyfriend wearing those."

"I'm not worried about that, Cynthia."

She snickered again. "Well, maybe it's all for the best. All men do is fill you up with hopes and dreams and then lie their asses off anyway. So take another piece of advice: stay single and stay a virgin." She cocked a brow. "You are still a virgin, right?"

"*Cynthia!*" I raised my voice.

"Hey, I'm just asking. Not trying to get in your business."

Cynthia fell silent for a moment then sucked her teeth. "You know what, don't listen to me. I'm just bitter. I'm sure your love life will turn out much better than mine."

"Look, I'm sorry about what happened between you and Greg."

Cynthia nodded while lighting up another cigarette. "Yeah, so am I. But I've learned one thing." She got teary-eyed. "A baby won't hold down a man—that's for sure."

Although I felt bad for Cynthia, a small part of me felt she was getting what she deserved. She selfishly left Aunt Harriet alone, for months, without a phone call just to chase a man who only treated her like shit in the end.

"So what are you going to do now?"

"I guess start working again, save up and find a place for me and Brandon."

"You don't want to live with Aunt Harriet? It would be a whole lot cheaper."

"Oh, no, I can't stay here for long. There's nothing out here for me. Besides, we need our own space."

Brandon started crying, and the sorrow on Cynthia's face was instantly replaced with a smile.

"Would you like to meet your nephew?" she asked, putting out the cigarette.

"Yes, of course I do."

Cynthia lifted little Brandon from the bed and placed him in my arms. He hushed when I began rocking him. "See. I knew you'd be a natural." She watched proudly.

As Brandon squeezed my finger, I thought about motherhood. It seemed to give Cynthia a kind of inner peace and warmth I'd never seen in her before. I wondered if it would do the same for me. Would it, one day, heal my broken spirit?

Part III

Chapter 37

May 1991

THE woman was a sadist! I was certain of it. If she yelled at me one more time to suck it in, I swear I'd take her own damn measuring tape and strangle her with it.

Mama made me come to this place—this house of horror disguised as a formal wear/alteration shop. But I knew the truth. Ana's Event was a store by day, but at night...I bet the basement was used for either strange sexual acts or as a torture chamber with Ms. Ana shouting at people in her Eastern European accent.

"Are we done yet?" I said with a serious attitude.

"This no good," she said bluntly. "Can't zip up—you need size twenty."

I shot her a fierce look then rolled my eyes because I didn't want to be here in the first place, and I definitely didn't need to hear that I'm fat. I already knew that. But Mama begged me to drive twenty-five miles away from home to try on dresses for a senior prom I knew I wouldn't attend.

"Mama, I'm tired of trying on dresses. Please, let's just go home."

"Okay, baby. I know you're tired. But do your old mother a favor—try on this royal blue dress for me. I promise it'll be the last one."

Mama looked up to me sweetly with her weathered eyes and excited grin. And of course, grudgingly, I gave in.

I put on the dress and then stared at myself in the dressing room mirror. It was a form-fitting dress with sheer blue arms and décolletage area. Even I had to admit the dress was pretty. But it only amplified the fact that my once pear-shaped figure was now looking more like an apple.

"Well, c'mon out and let us see," Mama shouted.

While I came out wearing a trace of a smile, Mama's face lit up like a Christmas tree.

"Oh, my heaven, you look so beautiful. I can just see you with your hair in a French roll."

"Very nice," Ms. Ana said.

"Mama, please, can we go now?"

"What's wrong? Don't you like it?" she asked.

I shook my head. "No."

Mama let out a disappointed sigh. "All right, Lovely, we can go."

I changed out of that costume faster than Superwoman. I didn't mean to be a bitch, but I felt I was being forced into something I didn't want.

Charging toward the exit, I heard Mama ask the woman to hold the dress for me.

"Normally, I don't hold," she replied. "But for you—two days."

The moment I pulled out of the parking lot, Mama started to lay on a guilt trip.

"You're going to regret this one day," she urged. "Last year you refused to go to the junior prom and here it is—your last chance, and you won't take advantage of it. These years don't come back, Lovely. I hope you know that."

"I know that, Mama," I said softly. "Don't you think I've thought of that many times?"

"Then talk to me, child. Why won't you go to your prom?"

"Because I don't have a date, that's why. Nobody wants to take a fat girl to the prom."

"Don't talk like that!" Mama said with a raised voice. "You know how I hate to hear you talk about yourself like that. You're a beautiful, beautiful plus-size girl."

"Beautiful to you, Mama, but not to boys my age."

"Have you seen Ruth Chamberlain's granddaughter? She's almost twice your size, and she has a boyfriend. I see them together in church all the time."

"Yes, I have, Mama. But she's also in college. I'm dealing with high school boys."

"Well, I still think you can get a date. You've got two weeks. I want you to go. And if your father was still alive, he would want you to go too."

And there it was. I was waiting on it. Anytime Mama wanted to reinforce her wishes, she'd mention what Daddy would say or do if he was still around. Daddy left this earth three long years ago, but it still hurt like it happened yesterday. I missed him so much. Sometimes I'd even turn on that Bob Ross painting show, turn up the volume, and pretend Daddy was watching it in the den while I washed dishes or cooked just to feel him. Somehow that brought me peace. But we were blessed not to see Daddy suffer. Before the cancer got really bad, God took him in his sleep.

"Lovely, what about Jamal, have you asked him to the prom?"

"No, I haven't."

"Well, why not? You two are close friends. He's the obvious choice."

"I think he has a date, Mama."

"You think? But you don't know that for a fact?"

"No, ma'am. But I'm sure he does by now."

Chapter 38

Four days earlier

IT felt like there was a volcano erupting in my intestines. The oatmeal and banana I ate for breakfast sent me running down the school hallway and into a bathroom stall before first period. Hoping no one would hear or smell me, I pulled down my panties then let it rip.

Ah, what a relief! I thought with my eyes closed.

The school bell rang. I knew hordes of girls would be entering any second to primp in front of mirrors to check their hair and makeup. So I started to push real hard to get it all out. But it was too late. Instantly, my feet went up when I heard voices.

"Kevin and I are wearing black and white to prom," I heard one girl say. "I can't wait for you to see my dress. I'm doing a 1920s theme."

"That sounds hot! Well, I'm wearing a purple fishtail dress. I gotta make sure I flaunt my shape because when I walk into the room, I want all eyes on me," the other girl said, snapping her fingers.

My legs were getting tired so I quietly set them down.

"Niecy, you are so crazy. You actually bought a dress even though y'all haven't made plans yet."

The moment I heard the voice and name, I twisted my lips out of sheer annoyance. It was Niecy King from my U.S. history class. She had such a big mouth to match her big tits and big behind. Boys didn't know whether to screw or fear her because she looked so grown for her age.

"Seriously, Niecy, the prom is only three weeks away. Are you sure Jamal Turner is going to ask you to the prom?"

Jamal Turner! I grimaced. *When did Jamal hook up with Niecy?*

"I'm absolutely sure," Niecy replied with confidence.

"I'm just asking because I heard he could be taking Lovely Duval to prom."

"Lovely Duval," Niecy hissed. "That fat bitch! I don't think so. Jamal told me that they are only friends. And trust— after we kissed, her name was never brought up again. Now just imagine what he'll do when I give him some on prom night."

"You are so wicked," the other girl said. Then they walked out.

I had been a victim of gossip and vicious name calling for years. Usually, it wouldn't faze me. But this time, the insult pierced right through my tough hide. I sat on that toilet and cried until my butt and thighs went numb. I never made it to first period.

Chapter 39

IN the driveway I heard rap music with thunderous bass. Mama flinched in her seat.

"What is that noise?" she said.

I looked in the rearview mirror. It was Jamal parked behind us, waving in a 1982 black Honda Civic Hatchback that he'd been talking about for the longest time.

I got out and gave Jamal an unamused stare while he stood in the doorway—all teeth and head bobbing. "Aren't you proud of yourself," I said, finally cracking a smile.

"Turn down that racket!" Mama shouted, closing the passenger door.

Jamal turned off the engine in a hurry.

"Sorry, Mrs. Duval, I just wanted to show off my new ride and sound system," he said, walking toward her.

With a smile, Mama put her hands on Jamal's arms. "Look at you, my handsome tall boy. You worked hard and got yourself a car, didn't you?"

"Yes, ma'am, I did."

"Now, you be careful on those streets. Watch those traffic signs and obey the speed limits, all right?"

"Yes, ma'am, I will."

"Good, good." Mama nodded. "Now tell me something, Jamal. Why haven't you asked my daughter to the prom?"

Jamal gave me a quick, wide-eyed glance, and I gave it right back, feeling blindsided.

"Well, Mrs. Duval, Lovely doesn't want to go to the prom. At least that's what she told me a long time ago."

"Boy, she only told you that because she doesn't have a date. Do you have a date, young man?"

"No ma'am."

I threw Jamal another perplexed look because I knew what I heard in that bathroom last week. He and Niecy were an item and heading to the prom.

"Well, y'all should go to prom together…problem solved."

Mama turned to me. "You see Lovely, all you had to do was ask. It took me less than two minutes to get you a date. Now you kids work out the rest on your own. I'm going inside to soak my feet in Epsom salt."

I caught Mama's eyes and cracked a subtle smile before she walked away.

"You really did it," I said, turning my attention to Jamal. "You finally raised enough money to buy that Honda Civic you've been salivating over for nearly a year. So, how does it feel?"

"It feels great," he said, rubbing his chest. "Working all those hours at Taco Bell was well worth it. Now I don't have to use Gerald's car or ask him to take me somewhere."

"Yeah, I hear ya. But I still can't believe that old man sold it to you for so cheap…twenty-one hundred bucks! I guess he really took a liking to you when you started mowing his lawn last year."

"I guess so," he agreed. "But I also know he's in a rush to sell all of his stuff before moving to that retirement home in Florida."

"Well, like I said before…your gain."

I locked the car door and walked over to Jamal.

"So, listen—about Mama. You really don't have to take me to prom. If you already have plans, I understand. She'll just have to get over it. Besides, prom is for her anyway. She just wants pictures."

"Actually, I don't have plans. I mean me and my boys, Quincy and Malik, talked about going stag and cruising around afterward, but that was just talk."

"Really, I'm shocked."

"Why is that?" he asked.

"Well, I heard you were going to prom with Niecy King. And you two sealed the deal with a kiss."

"Man, what is with that girl? I've been hearing that all week long. But I told Niecy I didn't want to go with her."

"So, what about the kiss? Was that true?"

"Yeah, I kissed her…but only when she kissed me first after a basketball game last month. Look, we are *not* a couple. If we were, don't you think I would of told you?"

"I don't know about that, Jamal. You didn't tell me about Trina back in tenth grade."

"Man, shoot. That doesn't count. I dumped that girl within a week."

I chuckled. "So what now?" I asked.

"That's up to you, Lovely. Do you want to go to prom with me?"

Even though we were just friends, his question made the hairs on my arm stand up. I thought I'd never hear those words come from a boy—let alone Jamal. I always shunned the idea of going to prom simply to protect my feelings from rejection. But I never stopped to explore the fact that, deep down inside, I really wanted to go.

And for the first time, I was beginning to feel what other girls felt: excitement.

"Yes, I do."

"Okay, cool. I guess we need to talk about our outfits. Do you have an idea of what colors we should wear?" he asked.

The dress at the shop flashed into my mind.

"How about royal blue and black?"

Chapter 40

THERE hadn't been this much fuss over me since I participated in the town's Little Miss Willisburg pageant back in the seventh grade. Yesterday Ms. Ana had me standing up for nearly forty minutes in one position to finish last minute alterations.

"Don't gain weight," she warned. "Because dress fits you perfect."

Then early this morning, Mama sent me to a beauty salon to get my nails painted and my legs and light mustache waxed. And now I was sitting in the kitchen, wrapped up in a pink robe getting my hard-pressed hair pinned up for tonight's senior prom.

"I think your French roll would look good with a bang. What do you think?"

"Yes, Mama, I think you're right. Let's try it."

As she passed me a mirror to check it out, I heard the screen door open then shut.

"Where's this dress I keep hearing about?" Aunt Harriet shouted.

"It's right there hanging on the bathroom door," Mama shouted back. "But don't touch it unless your hands are clean."

"What do you mean, unless my hands are clean? Of course my hands are clean."

"Just mind the dress," Mama commanded.

Aunt Harriet entered and looked over the gown. "That is a nice dress. Makes me remember when my Cynthia went to the prom. Remember, Dolores? She wore a gold and black mini dress."

"Yes, she was a beautiful sight."

"Speaking of Cynthia…guess what I got in the mail?"

Aunt Harriet started to open a big manila envelope she was carrying.

"Look at this picture!" She squealed.

It was a picture of Cynthia with her husband Robert, Brandon—now age three—and the new addition to their family: seven-month-old Robert Neely, Jr. Cynthia met Robert at a barbershop where she worked. They started dating. And this time, Cynthia made sure to introduce him to the family. We liked him a lot, but Aunt Harriet liked him even more. She said her prayers were answered when God sent her daughter a man with character and a good job with the Navy despite the fact he was eight years older and divorced. But what Aunt Harriet didn't like was when Cynthia and Robert ran off and eloped in Myrtle Beach. She felt cheated out of a wedding, so she settled for a backyard wedding reception instead. That was two years ago. They'd been living on a naval base in Japan since then.

Becoming a grandmother gave Aunt Harriet a new purpose in life and made her and Cynthia bury all hatchets. Nowadays, it seemed like Aunt Harriet only lived to spoil and talk about those boys. I knew the moment she got home, she wouldn't waste any time adding this picture to her shrine of grandbabies.

"Do you see how big they're getting, Dolores?"

"I see. I think Robert Jr. is looking more like his father the older he gets."

"Ain't that the truth? Oh, I can't wait to see them," Aunt Harriet said.

"Yes, we're all looking forward to that," I said, standing up. "Mama, I'm going to put my dress on now."

"Do you need some help?" she asked.

"No, I think I've got it."

After putting on some light makeup, I slipped into my shaper and custom-fitted dress. And just like Ms. Ana promised, it fit my body perfectly like a glove—magically smoothing out fat rolls and hugging my curves in all the right places. I had never seen myself so beautiful before and looking like a woman.

"C'mon on out here, girl. What you waiting on?" Aunt Harriet hollered.

I stepped out from my bedroom feeling like a confident queen.

"Look at my baby," Mama beamed. "Let me get my camera."

"Yes, ma'am, you look amazing," Aunt Harried agreed. "And look at those matching shoes."

"Ooh, I've got the perfect thing to make everything complete." Mama reached for a box on the table. "A girl at Claire's helped me pick these out."

"Oh, Mama, they're gorgeous."

"Yes, I know. Now put them on."

I put on the shimmering teardrop earrings and matching bracelet.

"How do I look?"

"Beautiful," Mama replied, her eyes shining. "Absolutely stunning just like I always knew you would."

I started to tear up. "Thank you, Mama. Thank you so much for convincing me to do this."

She nodded with a wide smile. And that's when a knock came at the door.

"Oh, that must be Jamal. Get your camera ready, Dolores."

Aunt Harriet opened the door. "Come on in. We've been waiting on you," she said.

Jamal walked in looking so handsome. His high-top fade and mustache were freshly trimmed. And his black and royal blue bowtie and cummerbund matched my dress perfectly.

"Lovely, you look...I don't know what to say. You look beautiful."

"And that's good enough," Mama said. "Come on in here and let's get a picture of you two standing side by side."

Jamal came in close and put his arms around me. I looked at our reflection in the mirror on the wall. No doubt we were an attractive pair. We just looked right together—like this moment was meant to be.

"Ooh...now this is a good one," Mama said, showing us the Polaroid.

"Yes, that is nice," I agreed. "Let's send one of these pictures to Anika."

"Yes, that's a good idea."

"Lovely, we better get going." Jamal chimed in. "Besides, my mom and Gerald want us to stop by so they can take pictures too."

"All right then kids, be safe and have a good time," Mama said. "But don't be coming back to my house at an inappropriate hour. Let's just set the curfew at 1:00 AM...deal?"

"Deal," Jamal and I said at the same time.

As we were walking toward the car, Aunt Harriet stepped on the porch and hollered, "And don't be bringing back no babies either."

Jamal and I looked at each other and started laughing

"Oh, hush up, Harriet. They're good kids. Now come on back in this house."

"Yeah, they're good kids. But they're also young and human too."

Chapter 41

AFTER taking pictures in the lobby, Jamal and I walked into the Greenwood Shriner's banquet hall like we owned the place. With our heads held high and looking our best, we commanded attention as we passed table by table until settling on one that wasn't occupied.

Jamal pulled a seat out for me and then placed it in front of the table. Scooting up his chair next to mine, he leaned into my left ear and then said, "I put you front and center for a reason. Look around. Do you see how everyone's looking at you?"

No way, I thought. But it was true. As I began to scan the crowed room, I noticed a group of girls across the hall chattering and looking my way, and then I saw Sabrina. We made eye contact and waved at each other. But what came next was *so* unexpected. I saw Zachary Finch, captain of the football team and Theo Huxtable lookalike, give me a double take. *I must be in a fairytale*, I said to myself, still finding it hard to believe people were looking at me out of admiration and not ridicule.

"Hey, let's go dance," Jamal said, snapping me out of my haze of disbelief.

"Right now?" I asked.

"Yes! We didn't come here to sit all night."

Jamal and I danced through five fast songs until finally a slow one came on. It was "Forever My Lady" by Jodeci, a very popular song—so popular that people rushed to the dance floor as soon as the melody started to play.

"Do you still want to dance?" I asked.

"Yeah, girl, this is my song!"

Jamal took my waist while I leaned into his chest. I chuckled inside because the last time I did this with a boy, my period started.

"Forever my lady," Jamal began to sing out loud.

"Boy, be quiet. You know you can't sing."

"Ha…neither can you," he laughed.

"Oh, so you got jokes tonight."

"Nah, that's not a joke. A joke would be: Why did the chicken cross the road? Your inability to sing, my dear, is a fact."

"Shut up you fool." I started to laugh then turned my head. And that's when I saw Miss Niecy King on the dance floor, giving me evil eyes in her skintight dress. *Yep, that's right. It's me…fat ass Lovely dancing with your fantasy man.* I simply responded by smiling because nothing or no one was going to ruin my night.

***

Moments after the prom king and queen were announced, the crowd began to thin out. So we left. It was still early at 10:05 PM, so we decided to take a thirty-five minute drive to the waterfront park in downtown Charleston.

We walked down a dark promenade that was illuminated by only a few street lamps and the moon above until we found an empty bench. The harbor was beautiful. The breeze, the sounds of seawater crashing against rocks, and the moonlight glimmering over the ocean made it the ideal backdrop for romance. And that's when a sobering reminder seeped in.

This is not a romantic date, Lovely.

"What are you thinking about, girl? It's like you've taken a trip to space."

"Ah, nothing," I said.

"Don't lie to me. I know what you were thinking about."

"You do?" I asked, surprised.

"Sure. You're wondering what you're going to do with the rest of your life."

"Well, that wasn't exactly what I was thinking about…but since you brought it up, what are you doing after graduation?"

"I guess get a job." He shrugged. "I just know college isn't for me. And I'm definitely not going into the military."

Jamal slid in closer with a smile on his face and a twinkle in his eye.

"You know, Lovely, I've got this fantasy about running off to New York and joining a jazz band. Who knows, maybe even start one of my own someday."

Jamal waved his hand across the starry sky. "Can you see it? Can you see my name in lights—Jamal Turner at the Apollo?"

"Yeah, I actually can see that," I agreed, smiling.

"And what's this about you going to Fordham Community College?" he turned and asked. "You're so smart. You could of gotten into any college you wanted, but you choose to downplay yourself. Like, why aren't you valedictorian?"

"I don't know, Jamal. I guess my heart just isn't into academics and going away for college. I just feel like I need to stay close to home to watch out for Mama. She's getting older, you know. Besides, I can get my prerequisites out of the way and then transfer to a four-year college any time I want."

He grabbed my hand. "Yeah, but will you do it?"

"What do you mean? Of course, I'm going to college."

"Well, I think you use your mother as an excuse not to go anywhere or do anything."

"That's not true."

"What! Last year, did you not give up the opportunity to visit the Biltmore Estates in North Carolina with the history class because you said that was too much time away from your mother?"

"Yeah, well, that trip also involved too much walking."

Jamal chuckled. "My point is, Ms. Dolores is not as needy as you think. And that makes me wonder. What's the real reason you're sticking around? Me—the first opportunity I get, I'm blowing this state." Jamal put his arm around me. "I'm just saying—you're smart, kind, and absolutely beautiful. The world could be yours...don't sell yourself short."

I sat there and soaked up everything Jamal said. He was right. I *did* lack ambition and had been selling myself short for years—doing exactly what I needed to get by, stay in my comfort zone and avoid attention, basically because I feared ridicule and being hurt by others.

Clearly, I took sabotaging myself way too far and lost a lot of my teenage years in the process. But I still had time to enjoy my youth because Jamal was here, staring me right in the face. He was my true love—the one who'd always been my friend, who gave me comfort in his arms when I felt pain, and now—encouragement. There was no doubt Jamal loved me and saw beyond my fat. He would never hurt me.

Sitting close to Jamal made my body warm everywhere. I knew I'd be putting our friendship at risk, but I felt a strong urgency to touch him. So I took a chance and quickly pressed my lips against his. But...he didn't kiss me back.

I pulled away and looked into his uninterested eyes. "You'll never love me—will you?"

"Lovely, I do love you." He shook his head. "But not in the way you want me to."

"I don't get it, Jamal. You've called me beautiful and smart so many times I've lost count."

"And you are...I'm just not attracted to you."

"Why not? Is it because I'm fat? Is it because I'm not built like Niecy King?"

"See, you didn't have to go there. It has nothing to do with any of that."

"Then why not me?" I pressed. "Why can't you be attracted to me? You've always overlooked me!"

"It's because I'm gay, all right!"

It felt like the wind had been suddenly knocked out of my lungs. My eyes began to water. I sprang up and rushed for the railings to catch my breath with Jamal following behind.

"I've wanted to tell you for the longest time," he said, placing his hand on my back, "but I just didn't know how."

I turned and gave Jamal a furious stare. "Look, save it! I've been rejected before. You don't have to make up a fucking lie—just to get me off your back."

"Lovely, I'm not lying."

"Take me home now, Jamal," I demanded, walking away.

"Lovely, please, just listen to me."

"I said take me home!"

Chapter 42

JUST like in Cinderella, my fairytale ball lasted only a few short hours. And then midnight came around and brought me back to reality. I felt like a cosmic joke. The universe had allowed me to experience some happiness and normalcy for once, and then snatched it away. Was God laughing at me in the heavens? Was I being tested for how much hurt I could endure?

I couldn't believe Jamal tried to sell me that jacked-up lie. It was bullshit! *Gay, my ass!* Ever since middle school, I watched him go through girlfriends like underwear. *No! No! No!* I seethed inside—slapping meat, cheese, and mayonnaise on bread in my prom dress. *Jamal just doesn't want me! I can't believe I wanted him to take my virginity tonight!*

I made two sandwiches, but I still wasn't satisfied even though I hadn't eaten one. So I grabbed a bag of Pizzeria chips, a pack of Oreo cookies, and a bottle of Sprite then headed for my bedroom.

"Lovely, is that you?" Mama hollered from behind her bedroom door.

I stopped in the hallway and took in a deep breath to compose myself.

"Yes, ma'am, "I answered.

"Did you have a good time?"

"Yes, ma'am, I did," I said, holding back tears. "But I'm tired now, Mama. Can we talk about this in the morning?"

"Okay, baby, goodnight."

Mama meant well. But I knew I shouldn't have gone to that prom. A tiny voice in the back of my head warned me that something, eventually, would go wrong. And it did. Why didn't I listen to that voice? What was I expecting putting my heart on the line? Too many times I had been either overlooked or rejected by guys because of my size. So what made me think Jamal Turner would be any different?

I nearly ripped off my fancy dress to get into my comfortable muumuu. Then in a hurry, I sat in the middle of my bed to spread out a buffet in front of me. And while tears streamed down my face, I took a hearty bite of a thick sandwich and then closed my eyes as it slid down my throat. Food was my pain medication—also my process to complete sedation.

Feverishly, I continued to eat even though I was no longer hungry and my guts felt like they could burst at any second. It was like my mind and body were working separately. I saw my hand repeatedly reach for food, but it seemed like my brain wouldn't stop it.

I forced myself to eat two more cookies until I couldn't swallow anymore. And then it happened. The sense of calmness I was waiting for finally kicked in followed by numbness. With drowsy eyes and my heart and mind depleted of all emotions and thoughts, I drifted backward onto a pillow. And my eyes settled on the digital clock. In less than one minute, I was knocked out.

***

Much later that night, I jumped out of my sleep with a sharp pain in my stomach and vomit in my mouth. Luckily, I had been lying on my side and hadn't inhaled and drowned. The pain was intense. So intense, I woke up Mama. Now we were in the emergency room talking to Dr. Lee.

"So, Lovely, let me get this straight," Dr. Lee said. "You didn't have any alcohol tonight after prom. But you did eat two sandwiches, a bag of chips, almost an entire pack of Oreo cookies, and then you washed it all down with a bottle of soda. Is this correct?"

"Yes, sir," I murmured with my head lowered.

"Well, no wonder your stomach hurts. That was too much food for any human to consume in one sitting."

"I told her that, Doctor," Mama said, shaking her head.

"So why did you eat all that food?" Dr. Lee asked.

Why? I could think of a lot of reasons why I overate. Number one reason...I wanted to escape. But I would never admit that to him. Not to a doctor who could put me in a loony ben.

"I don't know." I shrugged. "I guess I was just bored."

"Bored." He scoffed. "Listen, young lady, you need to find a much better, healthier activity to indulge in rather than binge eating." Dr. Lee rolled his stool closer to me. "Lovely, do you binge eat often?"

Our eyes met for a second. "No, sir," I lied again. The truth was I had stuffed myself many times before, but never like tonight—the amount I ate tonight even scared me.

"Well, for your sake, I hope you don't. Do you have any idea what binge eating can do to your stomach?"

I shook my head. "No, sir."

"It can rupture your stomach and lead to death."

"Oh, my lord. Please, Lovely, please tell me that's not what you're doing," Mama said.

"There's something else I want to bring to your attention. We checked your hemoglobin A1C and it read 6.0 percent. Do you know what that means?"

"No, sir."

"Well, it means you have prediabetes."

"Are you saying my child is going to have to start shooting up insulin?" Mama asked, sounding frightened.

"No ma'am," Dr. Lee replied, looking directly at Mama. "I'm not saying she needs to start medication at this time. I'm just saying that her blood sugar level should serve as a wakeup call. Because let's face the facts. No seventeen-year-old, at the height of 5'6, should weigh 240 pounds. I'm hoping with proper eating and exercise, Lovely can lose weight and avoid diabetes completely. You should have your daughter follow up with her primary physician within two weeks. But in the meantime, I'm going to recommend a good dietician I know. I hope you see her."

Mama looked straight at me when Dr. Lee mentioned a dietician. She knew exactly how I felt about them. The last one I had was mean, condescending and practically blamed me for all of my weight loss failures. I lost fifteen to twenty pounds with Slim-Fast shakes, Deal-A-Meal, Jenny Craig, and plain old exercise only to gain the weight back each time. I got so tired and frustrated of the diet seesaw. That's why I kept away from all those diet fads ever since.

Mama knew I wasn't going to see no dietician.

Chapter 43

I slept through Sunday morning and afternoon. I vaguely remembered Mama sticking her head in my bedroom door to ask me if I was all right. It was 4:35 PM by the time I decided to get out of bed. After taking a long pee, I slid into my flip-flops and then went outside to sit on the porch in my housecoat for fresh air. The mild breeze felt nice. The smell of Mama's collard greens was strong too. Then I heard the screen door shut and looked back.

"Lovely, how's your stomach feeling?" Mama asked, walking toward a rocking chair.

"It's better. I guess the medicine worked."

"Good. I'm glad to hear that." She nodded. "You know Jamal called a few times. I told him you weren't feeling well and that you went to the emergency room for your upset stomach."

"Oh, Mama, you didn't have to tell him all of that."

"Why not? He's your friend, isn't he? Besides, I told him you were all right. But he sounded real concerned so you ought to give him a call soon, okay?"

"Yes, ma'am."

"Lovely, you look so depressed. Are you going to tell me what happened last night? Did something happen at the prom? For heaven's sake, child, help me understand what drove you to eat all of that food."

I closed my eyes and let the tears fall while my mouth trembled in contemplation. I wasn't sure if I should tell her. But I had been holding on too many secrets already. So I turned around and let go of one.

"Jamal and I got into a horrible argument." I sniffled. "He lied to me, Mama."

"He lied to you about what?" she asked.

"Last night I told Jamal I had feelings for him. But he couldn't get into a relationship with me because..." I put my hand over my mouth and began to whimper.

"Because...what?" she pressed.

"Because he's gay," I whispered. "But he's a liar because I've seen him with girls before. Jamal just made up that stupid excuse because I'm fat and he doesn't want me." I took the end of my housecoat and wiped my face. "I feel like such a fool. I really thought Jamal was the one." I shook my head in defiance. "Well, he doesn't have to worry about me bothering him again. I'm done with being everybody's joke."

I looked at Mama's face. She appeared heartbroken but not shocked.

"Mama, did you hear what I said? Jamal lied to me about liking boys just to get rid of me and you don't seem surprised."

"Well, that's because I'm not surprised."

"What do you mean?" I asked, staring at her confused.

"I'm saying...I don't think the boy is lying to you."

"What!"

"Listen, honey. I've had my suspicions for years. The moment I saw him braiding your hair on this very porch, I just knew he was queer. But, I have to admit, I had been secretly hoping and praying, all this time, he'd grow out of those homosexual feelings. Because, like you, I thought you two would be perfect for each other." Mama sighed. "But I guess it's just not in the Lord's plan."

I still hung on to denial listening to Mama. The alternative was way too hard to accept.

"I can't believe you knew about him this whole time."

"Sure I did." She rocked back and forth in her chair. "That's why I didn't have a problem with Jamal climbing through your window at night."

I shot her a wide-eyed look. "You knew about that?"

"Of course I did, child. I know about everything that goes on in my house." Mama smiled at me warmly. "Lovely, I know you're hurt, disappointed, and was hoping Jamal would be your boyfriend. But you have to have faith that God has something better for you around the corner. Can you do that for me—try to believe?"

I nodded. "Yes, ma'am."

"Good. Now I need you to do something else for me. I want you to give Jamal a break and not be so hard on him. After all, I bet it took a lot of courage for him to tell you the truth. And I'm sure he's feeling pretty lonely without you."

"I guess you're right, but I just don't understand all of this, Mama. I mean, Jamal doesn't act or look gay."

"Now, I have to admit, I don't agree with or understand his nature either, but he's still a friend…right?"

"Yes he is," I answered with certainty. But then I began to wonder. How did I, Jamal's best friend, miss out on the signs? *What signs?* I thought. He never wore makeup. He never switched around or snapped his fingers in Z formation like those gay guys from "Men on Films."

"Mama, do you think his mother knows?"

"I'm sure she does. A mother knows about these things."

Mama started to cough.

"Are you okay?" I asked.

"Yep, I'm fine," she said then coughed again as she lifted her medium-size body out of the chair. "I'm going inside to put the cornbread on. Don't stay out here long."

Chapter 44

WEDNESDAY, June 5, 1991. It was the last day of school and my last day as a student at Willisburg High. Graduation was scheduled for this coming Friday and then my class would be ceremoniously set free to start our lives in the real world on our own terms.

The prospect of adulthood was exciting. There would be no more rules—no more supervision and being treated like a child. But I had mixed feelings walking down the student parking lot with my small box of memories in tow. Although I was glad to be leaving behind an authoritarian public school system, I just wasn't sure about what to do with my life.

Most of my classmates were thrilled about their futures and had mapped out plans. But me, on the other hand—not so much. I never gave my future a lot of thought beyond the next two years. I planned on working part-time at the grocery store and going to school at Fordham Community College, but that was as far as I got. Even on my college application, I checked *undecided* as a major.

When I was younger, I dreamt of becoming a teacher. Now, I felt unsure because I had no idea what I liked or wanted out of life. There were too many unanswered questions: Did I really want to be around kids all day? Would I even enjoy teaching? Without a doubt, I loved books. But did that make me a librarian like Mama? Mama told me to follow my own star. The problem was...I didn't have a compass.

I opened the car door and set the box on the back seat. Then I took a final scan of the football field and school building. That's when I heard bass thumping from a car behind me.

"I've been looking for you. Can we talk?" Jamal shouted.

I turned around to face him. "Sure."

He leaned over and pushed open the passenger door. "Do you mind getting in?"

I had been avoiding Jamal for two weeks. I spoke to him the day after I went to the emergency room, but we talked only about my health. I dreaded this conversation he wanted to have, but I knew it was necessary for us to move on.

Jamal parked in a secluded area in the parking lot. He was neatly dressed as usual in a crisp white V-neck T-shirt and beige shorts with brown sandals. And he smelled good too, like he had just come out of a fresh shower. *Oh, Lord, why is he gay?*

It took me the longest time to accept that fact, but over the last several days, my mind brought back the Annie T-shirt, the hair braiding sessions, and how he never tried to feel me up in my bedroom.

Silently I sat and looked straight ahead until he started the conversation.

"Lovely..." He cleared his throat. "I hope you know that I love you very much. And I wouldn't lie to you, especially about something that's been so hard for me to talk about."

I looked at Jamal's face; his eyes were glazed over with sincerity.

"I am so sorry if I ever led you on," he continued. "I never meant to hurt you."

"You've never led me on, Jamal. You've always made it clear that you only wanted a friendship from me. So the pain I feel is my fault. I'm the one who tried to change the rules. I took a chance and I lost." I shrugged. "That's life, right?"

Just as a few tears began to trickle down my face, Jamal wiped them away with his hand.

"I know it's difficult for you to believe it now, but I promise you there's someone out there for you. And he's going to be so much better than me."

"Now, that's hard to believe," I said through quivering lips. "Who else is going to see me the way that you do? I can't imagine caring for some other guy more than I care for you."

I threw my palms over my face and shook my head. "Are you sure, Jamal? Are you sure you're gay?"

"Yes, Lovely, I am."

"But you had girlfriends," I said, looking evenly into his eyes. "Some you've even made out with."

"I know, Lovely, I know! It wasn't right. But I only used those girls to either cover up my sexuality or for me to figure out who I really was. That's why I never dated you. I could of never played you like that...I loved you too much as a friend."

"But I still don't understand. How are you so certain that you're gay when you haven't even slept with a girl yet?"

Jamal blew out a long breath then said, "Because I've already had sex with a guy."

"What!" I exclaimed. "With who and when?"

Jamal paused and then said, "I hooked up with Quincy McNeil about a week before prom."

"Wait! Quincy McNeil is gay too? What the hell is going on? Is everybody gay?"

He sucked his teeth. "No, girl. There's only a few of *us* around here. So don't worry…you're safe."

Jamal started the engine.

I rolled my eyes. "Look, I wasn't trying to be nasty."

"Yep, I know. Listen, I've got to get ready for work. But, is this going to change our relationship? The thought of losing you would kill me."

I got quiet for a second in deep thought.

"No, I'm still your friend. But I can't tell you that I understand why you're choosing this life."

"I didn't choose this, Lovely. It just is."

"Well, I mean I don't understand your attraction to boys. Does that make sense?"

"Yeah." He nodded. "You're not gay, so that I can understand."

He put his foot on the brake and then put the car in gear. "Also, could you keep this just between the two of us? I'm not fully ready to come out yet and I haven't even told my mother."

"You haven't told your mama?"

"No, you're the first one I've told, besides Quincy. But I plan on telling her soon."

Jamal drove back to my car. Before getting out, he kissed me on the forehead and thanked me again for my friendship and discretion. To me our talk was bittersweet. For selfish reasons, I hated he was gay. But the upside to all of this...if I couldn't have him, at least no other female would.

Chapter 45

AUNT Harriet stood, excited, in front of her dresser mirror holding a pair of red culottes up to her waist. "Well, girls, what do you think?" she asked. "Cynthia told me that even though late June is the beginning of Japan's rainy season, I should still dress cool because of the humidity."

I gave Mama a quick glance before offering my opinion. "I think it's nice, and it's going to look even better with your black frilly blouse."

Mama nodded her head. "Yeah, I agree."

Mama and I were at Aunt Harriet's house to keep her from bouncing off the wall and help her pack for the trip next week. Cynthia figured it would be much cheaper to have Aunt Harriet visit her instead of lugging her entire family over here to the states. She sent her apologies to me and Mama, of course. Then she promised she'd come home as soon as the budget allowed so we could meet Robert Jr. too.

Aunt Harriet had never been out of the country or even out of South Carolina. Excitement was an understatement to describe her mood. It was almost as though she became a teenager all over again.

"If you liked that one, you should see the green and gold number I picked up from K-Mart yesterday," she said, flipping through hangers in the closet. "Ooh, but wait! Look at this."

Aunt Harriet pulled out a T-shirt with the biggest smile on her face. The T-shirt read *World's Greatest Grandma* on the front and *#1* on the back.

"You're going well prepared, aren't you?" Mama laughed.

"You know I am!"

We laughed and then heard a car horn beep repeatedly. "Who's that?" Aunt Harriet asked, walking over to the window. She pulled back the curtain. "Lovely, that's Jamal over there in y'all's driveway blowing his horn like that. Go see what's wrong with him."

I rushed home and met Jamal at the back of his car. He looked upset. I could tell he had been crying because his eyes were swollen and red. Through the rear windshield, I saw a suitcase and some boxes on the back seats.

"Where are you going?" I asked.

"Anywhere except here," he said through clenched teeth and flaring nostrils.

"Wait a minute...you're making me nervous. What happened, Jamal?"

He lowered his head and began shaking it slowly.

"Jamal," I said, "you've gotta tell me what happened."

"I got put out," he snorted and wiped his face.

"What do you mean, you got put out? Your mama put you out?"

"Nah, Gerald did."

"Why," I asked.

"Oh, you know why. I told them I was gay and in love with Quincy. That's when Gerald jacked me up against the wall and told me, 'No stepson of mine is going to be a fucking punk under my roof.' Mama tried to stop him, but Gerald went to my room and started throwing my stuff into a box. And that's when I was like 'Fuck it' and just finished packing myself while mother just sat on the living room couch crying."

"I am so sorry, Jamal," I said, touching his arm.

He dried his eyes and regained his composure. "Don't be, because this needed to happen. Everything is now all out in the open. Besides, I'm ready to leave. I will not tolerate Gerald putting his fucking hands on me."

"Well, you know you can always stay with me and Mama."

"I know, Lovely. And I appreciate that. But it's time for me to leave Willisburg. There's nothing here for me anymore."

"So, where will you go? What will you do?"

Jamal sighed. "I'm not sure what I'll do. And I guess I'll go wherever my little bit of money takes me."

I started to tear up. He put his hand on my face.

"Hey, don't worry about me. Once I get settled, I'll either call you or send you a letter."

I shook my head then fell into his chest.

"Oh no, Lovely, please stop crying." He rubbed my back. "Remember, I told you a long time ago I would never leave you. Well, I meant it. You believe me, right?"

I pulled away from his embrace and looked up. "Yeah, I believe you."

Before Jamal left, I gave him almost all of the money I had saved up in my lockbox. With no job and no place to live, I had a strong feeling he would need that $1,800 more than I would.

Chapter 46

I hated working during the holidays. The checkout lines were often long and too many times filled with antsy people who couldn't wait their turn to be rung up. I'd get all kinds of impatient stares. My favorite was the fuming, bug-eyed stare. Like I had control over customers who carried booklets of coupons or wanted a price check just to save ten cents. Nope, those types of customers did not faze me at all. While they gave their best displeased stares, I would just calmly continue to scan items thinking, *Tough Tittie. Stand in line and wait your turn just like everybody else.*

But the shopper who irked my nerves the most was the tabloid grazer. That was the person who'd zone out while reading something like the *Enquirer* and hold up the line—trying to read an entire magazine for free. And ever since Magic Johnson made the cover of every type of magazine by announcing he had HIV, grazing had gotten worse.

Not only did Magic's announcement shock the nation, it also forced me to think hard about Jamal on a daily basis. I hadn't heard from him since he left Willisburg back in June. He didn't even call to wish me a happy birthday last month, which had never happened.

I wondered so many times how he was and where he'd be spending his Thanksgiving and Christmas holidays. But, most of all, I wondered if he was healthy.

"Lovely, your tip for grits was a hit with my family," Ms. Judy, a regular customer I sometimes shared recipes with, said. "I never thought adding heavy cream to grits would make my boys literally lick their bowls. Listen—If you ever decide to open up your own restaurant, let me know because my family and I are going to be your first customers."

"Oh thanks, Ms. Judy. That was sweet of you to say. You know I love to cook, but I'm not too sure about running a business."

As I handed her the receipt, a black lady I caught staring at me a few times from the back of the line finally made it to the front. She was conservative looking and may have been in her early to mid-forties. There was nothing really remarkable about her except she had long dark hair and wore big glasses on a thin, heart-shaped face. I had no idea who she was. But as she began to unload her buggy, she continued to give me glimpses. It made me so uncomfortable it forced me to say something.

"Do you know me, ma'am?" I asked with a friendly smile while ringing her up.

"I'm sorry. What did you say?"

"Do we know each other?" I asked again, still smiling. "I noticed you looking at me and my name badge. That's why I asked."

"Actually, I think I do know you. Aren't you Dolores and Joseph Duval's daughter?"

"Yes, I am," I said with an inquisitive squint. "How do you know them?"

"Oh, I used to go to Mt. Moriah Baptist church many years ago. And I just happened to be at your baptism that Sunday. Your name is very unique. Who could ever forget get it? Now, don't you have a sister as well?"

"Yes, ma'am, I do. Her name is Cynthia."

"Right." The woman nodded. "And has she grown up to be as beautiful as you are?"

"Well, thanks," I chuckled. "Even though I consider Cynthia to be much prettier than me. But, doing fine. She's married now and has children of her own."

"Oh how wonderful!" The woman beamed. "And your parents—how are they?"

"Well, Daddy died several years ago, but my mom is still going strong."

"Oh, I am so sorry to hear about Mr. Duval. I didn't know. I've been away for a while."

"Yeah, so am I. Do you remember my sister, Irene? She passed away too."

The woman nodded. "Yes, I remember her. And that was some heartbreaking news."

I scanned the last item and then pushed the subtotal button. "Your total is $24.59, ma'am."

The woman looked sad as she pulled twenty-five dollars out of her wallet. I gave her the change then asked, "What is your name?"

"What?" she replied wide-eyed as though I caught her off guard.

"I wanted your name so I can tell my mom you asked about her."

"Oh, that's okay." She shook her head and dropped coins into her purse. "She wouldn't remember me anyway." The woman walked off then suddenly stopped and looked back.

"You take care of yourself," she said in an odd intense way.

I nodded my head thinking, *What was that about?*

Chapter 47

MAMA greeted me at the front door with a giant grin on her face. "Look what finally came for you," she said, holding up a letter in her hand. It was from Jamal. *If this is supposed to be my long awaited birthday card, it's more than a month late!* I caught a quick attitude. But then I remembered, when dealing with Jamal…late is always better than never.

Walking past Mama, I took a seat on the living room couch and opened the light blue envelope that had Jamal's full name on it but no return address.

Curious…quite curious.

"Well, what did he send you?" Mama asked.

"Looks like a birthday card and a post card from New Orleans."

"New Orleans!" Mama exclaimed. "How did that boy get all the way over there?"

I shrugged. "I'm not sure. Your guess is just as good as mine."

Mama stood there staring at me with hands on hips, like she was waiting for me to read out loud. But I raised my eyebrows and gave a tight-lipped smile instead.

She got the hint. "Oh, let me give you some privacy."

When Mama walked away, I began to read the post card.

Nov. 24, 1991

Hey Lovely,

I'm so sorry for not contacting you sooner. I've been really busy. But at least I didn't forget your birthday. Well, sort of. I bet you're shocked to learn that I am now living in New Orleans. Trust me; I still think it's a dream. I followed Quincy down here. He's in college. And I work as a waiter during the day and then play my trumpet at clubs at night. Yeah, it's a lot of work but worth it! Listen, I just wanted you to know I'm okay. I will be moving to a new apartment soon, so I'll contact you. Happy Holidays, Jamal.

Walking toward the kitchen, I began to feel even lonelier and more aimless than ever. While Jamal was out in the world living his dreams, I still lacked passion for something and had no real direction in life. I began to wonder—was there anything out there for me at all?

"So, how's Jamal doing?" Mama asked while stuffing the turkey for the next day's Thanksgiving dinner.

"I guess he's fine," I said, sitting down at the table. "He's got a job as a waiter and playing his trumpet at a few clubs—sounds like he's happy."

"I'm glad to hear he's happy and making his own way. But I sure hope Jamal and his mother are back on speaking terms because it just breaks my heart to think they haven't spoken to each other in all this time."

The phone rang.

"Get that for me, Lovely."

"Hello?"

"Put ya mama on the phone," Aunt Harriet said, urgently.

"Okay, hold on." I stretched the phone to Mama.

"Who is it?" she asked, wiping her hands on a dishcloth.

"It's Aunt Harriet and she sounds serious."

Mama took the phone. "What is it, Harriet? What's wrong?"

She was silent as she listened to Aunt Harriet on the other end.

"Oh Jesus!" she cried out, reaching for a chair.

Quickly, I pushed a chair behind her. "Mama, what's going on?" I asked, my heart racing like wild horses.

"Aha, aha, mhm, oh my god," she moaned over the telephone and then finally hung up.

Watching tears roll down Mama's face made my body feel jittery. I didn't want to hear the bad news, but I needed to know. So I braced myself.

"Mama," I said while she collected herself, "what's wrong?"

"It's Nathan." She sniffed. "He's dead."

My heart sank into my stomach the moment I heard the word *dead*. I felt a barrage of emotions, but truthfully, grief was not one of them. I placed my hand on Mama's shoulder not knowing what to say except, "How did he die?"

"The police found his body in a crack house. So most likely, he died from an overdose."

"How long do they think he's been dead in that house?"

"They don't know. His body was so badly decomposed, they had to cremate him. The police said if it weren't for his dog tags, Nathan probably would have never been identified."

Mama took a couple of deep breaths. "I'm all right. I'm all right." She rubbed her chest. "You know I think I've always known Nathan would succumb from his addictions. But, still, I had hope for him. After all, he was my baby brother."

"I'm going to get you a warm washcloth for your face, Mama. I'll be right back."

She let out another sigh and then nodded.

In the bathroom, I twisted the rag in my hand, still feeling stirred inside. My uncle, also the source of my torment, was dead. It hurt me to see Mama so sad, but I couldn't grieve for Uncle Nathan. Not one tear left my steely eyes.

I gazed at myself in the mirror, wondering. Was I evil for feeling not a thing? *No*, I answered in thought. He interrupted my childhood with no real remorse. As far as I was concerned, this was justice. And all was well with my soul.

Chapter 48

Fall 1996

I don't remember exactly when I fell in love with the art of cooking. It had to be somewhere between the time I discovered Julia Child's cooking shows on PBS and taking my first free cooking class back at Fordham Community College where I learned how to dice an onion like a pro and make a proper rue. Either way, it seemed like a light switched on in my head after those experiences. And for the first time in my life, I had clarity and felt excitement about something I truly enjoyed.

After I transferred to the College of Charleston to finish my bachelor's degree in business administration in the spring of 1995, I took a year off from academia to find myself. For about a month, I continued to do book keeping at Piggly Wiggly full-time, but on Saturdays I went to cooking classes. I loved those cooking classes. I loved them so much I ended up taking on a part-time job as a prep cook at Kelsey's Steakhouse just to get some real world experience. The money sucked—that was for sure. But it helped me make a decision. I decided to bypass a MBA to pursue an associate's degree from Johnsons & Wales Culinary School of Arts instead. That way I could land a job as a chef, a restaurant manager, or even open my own business one day.

In hindsight, I guess Ms. Judy and Mama really had crystal balls and saw me going into the food industry. But I had no clue. Yep, on the surface, it seemed like I had it all. I earned a bachelor's degree with honors and had a promising career to look forward to, but a love or social life…not so much. I never made significant friends in college, nothing like I had with Anika or Jamal. And even at the age of twenty-two, soon to be twenty-three in a few weeks, I still wasn't dating. In fact, I was still a virgin. A predicament I thought would never last this long—but I was absolutely wrong.

I vividly recall the day when Anika called me up to tell me she had lost her virginity to a guy named Mike. It was the day after her nineteenth birthday. She passionately described the night as being romantic and explosive at the Holiday Inn. *Shoot!* After listening to that, I couldn't wait until I had my first roll-in-the-hay too. It even made me start doing my hair on a regular basis and wearing more fashionable clothes just to catch a man. Oh, I managed to get a few flirty smiles and stares from married or older men. But I never got attention from men I found datable. I didn't think I was picky. I just wanted someone who had good teeth, nice hair, was tall, handsome, well-groomed, had a degree or working toward a degree, was smart, well-mannered, kind eyes, ambitious, and not too fat because I imagined two fat people couldn't do anything in the bedroom.

It was all too depressing how my efforts wouldn't bear fruit. I did everything to put myself on the market except go club hopping, which never had been my thing in the first place. And I definitely wasn't into this new trend on campus of meeting guys in online chat rooms. That was just a murder waiting to happen. So, over time, I painfully accepted the fact that having nice hair and a pretty face just wasn't enough to attract a man. Apparently, I needed to have the body to match—and Lord knows, at 260-ish pounds, I continued to struggle in the weight department.

I sometimes made fun of my situation to Mama's dislike. Last year, on my birthday, I refused to go out and celebrate. "Go where and with whom? I don't have any close friends in town," I told her, chuckling. "Besides, I've already purchased my one way ticket to Spinsterville." Humor was one of my defense mechanisms, but Mama detested those comments. She told me I was just a late bloomer and that kind of talk was going to get me nowhere fast. But I wasn't that pessimistic and blind. Surely I'd seen plus-size women walking around with good-looking men before. So I knew it was possible. It's just I hadn't been able to snag one of those chubby chasers for myself.

In all seriousness, though, if Jamal were here, I'd ask him, "What's wrong with me? Or, what I am I doing wrong?" And no doubt, he would give me the straight-up truth from a male's—although gay—perspective. But Jamal wasn't here. In fact, I hadn't heard from him in almost three years. From the last letter he sent, I learned he broke up with Quincy over money issues and had already found someone new—some thirty-year-old musician he met on the road. They were supposed to be living in California together. But who really knew? The letter had no return address and his mother hadn't heard from him either. So only God knew where Jamal was and how he was doing. But I was certain I hadn't seen the last of him. He'd pop up someday.

And, as for me—I was excited. Today was orientation day. My new adventure into the world of culinary arts would start as soon as I parked my car.

***

First day jitters were definitely in play. I checked out the neatness of my uniform multiple times in the bathroom before settling my nerves and finally entering the kitchen. Pots and pans hung from chains. Stainless steel appliances and professional grade gas stoves lined the back wall—I was in a chef's heaven. I actually felt like I belonged when I laid my personal knife kit on a long table surrounded by fifteen other students.

I stood next to a woman whose skin was almost as dark as mine but her hair was long and silky black. We were two of only five people of color in the class. There were three females in total. But, the majority of the class was dominated by white men.

I grew restless waiting for the professor to walk in so I smiled hard at my neighbor.

"Hi," I said to her. "My name is Lovely."

"Hey." She returned a friendly smile. "I'm Olive Garcia, but you can call me Ollie."

"Olive—I like that. How did your parents come up with your name?"

"Actually, it was my mother's idea. She used to have a thing for olives." She chuckled. "Especially in martinis. So I guess when I popped out, she took one look at me and said, 'Olive!' But my dad—he wasn't so keen on the name, so he started calling me Ollie and it stuck."

"Wow, she really did love olives. So, do you have a thing for them?" I asked.

"Oh, no." She cringed. "I absolutely hate those things."

"I guess I would too."

"And what about you, is there a story behind your unique name?"

"No, I'm afraid not." I shrugged. "It's just a name."

"Hello everyone and welcome," the professor said, walking in. "My name is Chef Arnold, and this is Cooking Class 101. You may address me as Chef or Chef Arnold."

Ollie turned to me with an enthusiastic grin. "Here we go," she said.

For the next two hours, Chef Arnold went over kitchen rules and the fundamentals of cooking. I never knew cooking could be so technical. The good news was Ollie and I seemed to hit it off right from the start, so we decided to become partners in our classes. That took a lot of anxiety away. Plus, it was nice to have a potential new friend.

Chapter 49

MAMA had been coughing for the longest time. We noticed her ankles were swelling. Her primary doctor was concerned about Mama's weakness so he referred her to a cardiologist. The echogram test revealed she had congestive heart failure caused by damaged heart muscles.

We were returning home from the doctor's office. I slowly helped Mama walk up the steps and into the bed. For the first time, Mama looked old to me with the blanket pulled all the way up to her thin face. Her hair was white. And her eyes appeared dim. I just never thought she could get sick.

"Mama, are you comfortable?" I asked.

"Yes baby," she said quietly. "Now don't you worry about me. I'll be all right. You go on and study."

I nodded and gave her a kiss. Then after turning off the lights, I looked back and said with quivering lips, "I love you Mama."

In the hallway I threw my hands over mouth and was just about to break down when the phone rang. It rang twice more before I could reach it in the kitchen.

"Hello," I said, sucking up my tears.

"How's your mother?" Aunt Harriet asked.

"Tired…she's in the bed sleeping."

"Okay, I won't bother her then. So what did the doctor say?"

"He said she has congestive heart failure."

"What! Oh my Lord. So what does that mean, Lovely?"

"It means her heart isn't pumping blood efficiently and it's irreversible. But the doctor said medicines, exercise, and changing Mama's diet could stop her condition from worsening."

"So they ain't going to do some type of surgery on her?"

"No ma'am," I said. "There's nothing more that can be done right now…only monitor."

"Oh, Jesus. Well, tell ya mama I'll be there when she wakes up."

"Yes ma'am," I said, trying not to cry.

I hung up the phone with my hand on my stomach. It seemed like all my stress and anxiety went straight there. With tears flowing down my face, I grabbed a bottle of chocolate milk and rushed to my room to get a bag of sweets from the closet. *I can't lose Mama* was the mantra repeating in my head as I gulped and threw food down my throat in an attempt to dull my pain and silence those thoughts. But near the peak of my ravenous rage, I caught a glimpse of myself in the mirror. *What a disgusting sight!* Crumps outlined my lips and there was milk dribbling down my double chin. I put the cup down. Feeling nauseous, I broke out into cold sweat then vomited into the wastebasket.

This has got to stop. Why am I such a glutton? I need help.

A couple of months ago, I saw a flyer back at school calling on those who wanted to participate in Overeaters Anonymous. A few times I stopped in front of those flyers and questioned if that was me. And of course, I blew it off thinking my actions didn't fall into that category. But now, I was thinking differently. I recognized I may have a problem. I couldn't keep eating until I burst when something really hurt me.

Something had to change.

Chapter 50

THE Overeaters Anonymous meeting was held at a community center in North Charleston on a wintry Saturday afternoon. To my surprise, the room didn't look anything like how I imagined group therapy would be from television shows. There were no crazy-looking people sitting in a circle on metal chairs and the room wasn't drearily dark. Room 12 actually had a warm cozy feeling with a couch, a few rocking chairs and a recliner, and plenty of small throw pillows. The coffee maker in the kitchenette also gave it a homey touch.

I took a seat in a rocking chair and placed a pillow on my lap. I'm sure I grabbed the pillow for security being in an unfamiliar place. There were seven of us, including the counselor. I assumed the attractive black woman with dreads was the counselor because she was the only one with a name badge. The rest of the group was made up of five girls and one guy, all of us appearing to be in our early twenties and overweight, well—except for one girl, she was quite slim. I actually wanted to toss her a ham sandwich.

"Hello everyone," the woman said. "My name is Rita Malone and I am a group counselor for Overeaters Anonymous. I hold a doctorate in behavioral psychology and I am collecting data for research on this subject matter. Now, I want you guys to be at ease. These sessions are strictly confidential. So, please, use first names only—doesn't matter if they're fake or real."

I breathed out a sigh of relief when she said our names would remain private and by the looks on two other girl's faces, I wasn't alone.

"Does anyone have a question at this time?" She smiled wide.

"Yes, Dr. Malone, I do," a girl said.

"Oh, please, everyone just call me Rita. These meetings are very informal. But, go ahead. What's your question?"

"Okay. Um, are these sessions going to be videotaped?"

"No, absolutely not. Listen guys, this is a safe zone. So please feel free to share and speak your minds. There are no judgments here. Are there any more questions?"

Rita paused to give everyone time to respond.

"Okay then," she continued. "For those of you who are new, at the last session I asked everyone to start a food journal to record how you felt before, during, and then after eating. I also asked you to write down your earliest memory of food binging because dealing with the origin of the problem is the best way to modify your behavior. Is there anyone who's ready to share?"

"I'd like to start, Ms. Rita," said the skinny girl.

"Okay, Jennifer, go ahead and start us off."

"Well, as you already know, I've been struggling with my past. You know, never really wanting to go there. But I did it again this week. I ate a large pizza with a thirty-two ounce big gulp in one sitting."

"Why did you do that, Jennifer?" Rita calmly asked. "What triggered that action?"

"Anger," Jennifer simply said.

"So, what caused the anger?" Rita asked.

Jennifer blew out breath. Her face looked flushed.

"I saw my stepmother again and it made me angry. My father didn't tell me he was coming to visit with her. And he knows how I feel about her."

"What happened between you and your stepmother?" Rita asked, passing a box of tissue.

"When I was a kid, my stepmother started putting me in beauty contests. I really didn't like them but my dad said they would give me confidence and teach me how to be competitive in the world. So I tolerated those pageants knowing it would make him happy and proud of me. But when I didn't win or place or even if I gained a little weight, I'd get cursed out or a pinched arm from my stepmother and my father would basically make up excuses for her."

Jennifer stopped to dry her eyes.

"I actually do remember the first time I binged. I was twelve years old, and I had just failed to place in another pageant. And of course my stepmom called me fat, a loser and other things. So that night, I discovered the wonders of food while everyone slept. I found out that food took the edge off. That was also the night I declared I wouldn't compete in a pageant again. And I didn't. But I continued to use food to soothe my hurt and anger—even today. But, nowadays, after binge eating I feel so guilty, I end up working out for hours just to stay thin."

"Jennifer, why didn't you tell your real mom about your stepmom?" a guy asked.

"I never knew my mom. She died from cancer when I was three."

"I want to thank you, Jennifer, for being brave enough to share your story," Rita said. "I know it wasn't easy…"

Rita continued to talk, but my thoughts were running so wild her words became faint in the background. I was thinking how my story wasn't so different from Jennifer's when it came to using food to soothe the pain. But I wasn't ready to share my story just yet. I knew the source of my pain. I just didn't know how to get past the shame.

Chapter 51

OLLIE and I won the spring bake-off for our class with a Limoncello cream cake and a strawberry with chocolate glazed tart. I was absolutely thrilled by the win because I had never been a strong baker in the past, and quite frankly, I never cared for it. But when Ollie started giving me tips in the baking and pastry labs, all of that changed. I began to love baking desserts and pastries.

We decided to celebrate our victory at Applebees in downtown Charleston. The bake-off finale signaled the end of the spring semester. And that meant no more classes until mid-July. I was beyond tired from all of my studies, taking care of duties at home, plus helping one day a week in the business office at Piggly Wiggly. Clearly, I needed a night out.

Ollie and I had become real friends over the last several months. I learned she was twenty-six years old, in the Army Reserves and was the proud single mother of a five-year-old girl named Mia. Mama got a kick out of Ollie's real name. And the instant she laid eyes on little Mia, she fell in love. I enjoyed meeting Ollie's parents as well, especially her mother. The first time I met her, I found it amusing how she squeezed Ollie's cheek then said, "And how's my little Olive today?" But Ollie was no Mama's or Daddy's little girl. When she got dumped by Mia's father, who'd been M.I.A. ever since she was born, she kept it moving and handled her own business. That's why I admired her. Not only was she a talented chef and fun to be around, she was also ambitious, courageous, and optimistic— something like how I used to be in my younger years...way before life tore me down.

I walked into Applebees a little after 7:00 PM to spot Ollie flagging me down.

"Hey, girl," she said when I reached the table. "What's your poison for the night?"

"Oh, I'm not drinking tonight," I said.

"What are you talking about, chica? School is out. Why don't you live a little?" she said, flagging down a server.

"Yeah, but I've got to work tomorrow."

Ollie shot me an annoyed look. "One drink isn't gonna hurt you, Lovely. Look, just get one margarita so we can toast to a successful year of culinary school."

I nodded my head with a smile. "Okay, just one margarita."

As soon as the server stepped away with our orders, Ollie started waving again.

"Who are you waving at?" I asked, looking back.

"Some guys from school, you know Hank and Isiah."

"Yeah, I've seen them before, but I don't know them."

"That's because they're in the bachelor's program," she answered. "You really need to mingle, Lovely."

"Well, they're coming this way," I said, turning back around.

"How's it going, Ollie? Yeah, what's up girl?" The guys stopped as the hostess was leading them to a table.

"I'm great," Ollie replied. "So, what are y'all up to tonight?"

"Nothing much," the white guy answered. "We're just here to get some food and beer."

"Okay. Cool. Well, have you two met my friend, Lovely? Lovely, this is Hank," she said, pointing to the white guy. And this African prince is Isiah."

"Aw, stop it, Ollie." Isiah smiled. "I see you've been watching *Coming to America* again."

"Ha!" Ollie laughed out loud. "You're right."

"You know, I've seen you a few times around campus. It's very nice to meet you," Isiah said to me with his hand extended.

I shook his hand. "It's nice to meet you as well."

Our server came back with our drinks.

"Now those look good ladies," Hank said. "Hey, the hostess is trying to seat us, so we'll see you later, Ollie. It was nice meeting you too, Lovely."

"Yes, it was very nice meeting you," Isiah said.

And just as they walked away, Ollie shot me a devilish stare. "Did you hear Isiah's sexy ass accent? And did you see his gorgeous smile? Woo! Girl, I wish I could snag him. But…he's not interested in me."

"Why would he not be interested in you? You're pretty."

"Girl, are you that blind or just naïve?"

I curled a brow. "What's that supposed to mean?"

"Lovely, the man does not want me because he wants you."

"What!" I gave her a shocked look. "Come on. How did you get that from a five-second encounter?"

"Girl, I know you haven't been in a relationship in a very long time. But surely you do know when a man is flirting with you…right?"

Actually, I've never been in a serious relationship before, I thought.

"Ollie, I'm not sure what you saw. But I am certain a good-looking guy like that was not flirting with me."

"Oh my God! Isiah practically lit up when you shook his hand. And what do you mean…a good-looking guy like that wouldn't be flirting with you? You've got beautiful hair and such a pretty face. Why—"

"Yeah, I've got some beautiful hair and a pretty face," I interrupted. "Ollie, I've heard that all of my life. But who are we kidding? My body is hideous. I'm fat! And nowadays, that's all that matters."

"Damn, Lovely," she said in a saddened voice. "That's how you feel about yourself—because you're heavy, you're not worthy of love? No wonder you've been alone for such a long time."

I picked up my strawberry margarita and took a gulp.

"Yeah, well—you have no idea how hard it is being my size. Not all women are lucky enough to have a body like yours, you know."

"What are you talking about? Listen girl, not all men want the same thing. There are men out there who prefer full-figured women. But nobody is going to love you if you can't love yourself first and project some confidence. And, seriously, if you're so dissatisfied with the way you look, then do something about it."

After that conversation, I ordered another drink.

***

Later that night I lay in bed thinking about what Ollie had said. Her words rang true and loud like an alarm clock, but those words were easier said than done. So many times I tried to lose weight with diet and exercise only to fail in the end. That's why I just gave up.

Ollie also said I needed to love myself. Well, I thought I loved myself. But maybe I didn't as much as I should. Many times I picked myself apart in the mirror, hating what I saw. Why couldn't I see what others said about me? Why couldn't I see myself as beautiful and love me in my own skin?

I got out of bed and stood in the mirror determined to see something nice about my body. I untied my hair and let it fall past my shoulders. Then I got naked. As I scrutinized myself, I cupped my D-size breasts. I liked their shape and fullness. For the same reasons, I liked my round butt. Next I moved on to my stomach—the area I hated the most—and ran my hands over rolls of fat and stretch marks. I closed my eyes, still feeling disgust. But I fought the demon within and told myself those rolls and stretch marks were mine.

"You're beautiful, Lovely," I murmured. "You are beautiful."

Chapter 52

I sat in the Overeaters Anonymous meeting nervous as hell. After attending several sessions, I decided today would be the day I'd share my story. The usual people were present, except Jennifer. We hadn't seen her for two consecutive sessions. Maybe she made a breakthrough. Maybe she no longer needed counseling because her pain was now off her chest.

God, I hope I make a breakthrough.

"So who would like to start off today?" Rita asked.

Slowly, I raised my hand. "I would."

"Okay, Sarah," she said, using my fictitious name.

"Um. Several weeks ago, I realized I had a problem with eating. And now, because of coming here, I know I'm an emotional overeater."

As I started to tear up, Rita passed me the communal box of tissue like it was a baton. I knew it was my turn to spill my guts.

"It's all right, Sarah. Take your time," Rita said.

I hung my head low, trying to find strength to continue and say the right words. Then I thought about it. Every person in this room had courageously shared their trauma and secrets with me. So why couldn't I?

I took a deep breath. "I remember exactly when I started overeating," I continued. "When I was thirteen, my uncle came to live with my aunt who lives across the street from me. At first I thought he was cool. He brought so much life to our lives after my sister died. But, eventually, I found out he was nothing more than a perverted bastard.

"One night I was sent over to get medicine for my aunt. While there, I heard horrible snoring coming from my uncle's bedroom. I went in to check on him to make sure he was okay. He seemed all right, but I noticed his penis hanging out of his boxers. Now you gotta understand, this was a shock for me. Being raised up by older parents in the country, I didn't know much about boys or sex. And I definitely had never seen a real penis before. I don't know why I did it. I guess curiosity. But I poked it with my finger. Well, he must've been watching the whole time, because the moment I pulled away, he grabbed my hand, put it on his penis, and then began jerking off.

"I begged him to stop—I really did. And even though it only lasted a few seconds, it felt like an eternity to me. I was so ashamed and embarrassed after that. I couldn't tell anyone. How could I? How could I tell my mom and aunt that their precious baby brother made me rub his dick? They wouldn't believe me—especially since I was the one who 'initiated' it. And that's when I started eating everything in sight. 'If I gain weight, no old man will ever touch me again,' I told myself. Well, I did a fantastic job of that because I've been fat ever since then…and alone. So even today, when something causes me anxiety or pain, I use food to calm myself down and go to sleep. That's how I escape from the world."

Holding a pillow to my chest, I started crying and rocking back and forth.

"And you've been holding that in for all these years?" Rita asked.

"Yes, ma'am," I said through my tears. "I'm messed up, right?"

"Sarah, you've been through a very serious, painful event—molestation by a family member is devastating. Trust has been broken and lines have been crossed. So you sedate yourself with food just to cope. But, with proper counseling, you will get through this and heal. And opening up and telling us your truth today was a major step in mending your mind, body, and soul. But, there's one thing I want you to know right here and now: you are not the villain in this. Now...it was not a good idea for you to touch your uncle's penis, but you were the child and he was the adult. He had no right taking it to the next level. And actually, what he did was downright criminal. Tell me something. Is he still around the family?"

"No, ma'am." I shook my head. "He died years ago."

"Okay. Well, like I said. I believe you can heal, but first you must let go of the guilt created by a thirteen-year-old, curious girl. Because if you don't release this festering guilt, the essence of your past will remain in your present and, ultimately—destroy your future."

After the session ended, I got into my car and cried one last time before returning home. I couldn't believe I just told a group of strangers about my deep-seated shame. But I was better for it. I felt lighter and more at peace. Rita was right. If I didn't let go of my pain, it would just consume me and fuck up my future. For too many years I wrapped myself up in a blanket of fat for protection—believing my life sucked and good things would never happen to me. *Well, I am worthy of blessings*, I thought. *I'm ready for a change!*

Part IV

Chapter 53

Winter 1998

I *am walking down the aisle in a big, grand church. My long lace veil trails behind me with on-lookers on their feet admiring my white form-fitting dress. I am absolutely stunning. And my groom at the altar, well—he's fine as hell.*

"Lovely," Anika called my name, interrupting my fabulous daydream. "Are you going to dance? Or are you going to just sit there the entire night?"

"Anika, I promise. I will dance, but not right now. I'm still trying to digest my food."

Anika gave her eyes a squint and pointed her finger. "All right, I'll leave you alone for now. But, remember—you promised."

"Okay, okay," I assured her. "You have my word."

It was not my wedding day. That honor belonged to Anika. She was beautiful in a champagne cocktail dress she changed into for the reception. It went well with her crimson-and cream-colored theme that was inspired by her sorority colors. It was also perfect for a Valentine's Day wedding at the elegant Sterling Ballroom on Hilton Head Island in South Carolina. I wished Mama could see Anika in person. She'd be so proud. But her health wouldn't allow the long, exhaustive drive.

Life can be so unpredictable at times. That's what popped in my mind watching Anika dance with her new, handsome husband. I never thought, in a million years, she would become a schoolteacher and get married to a vice principal of a high school. I always imagined her traveling the world as a singer and living it up. But she chose to skip fame and fortune when she fell in love and sang only in churches now. But I knew she was happy. I could feel it.

"Hey, young lady," said an older man sitting next to me at a table. His thin body, short stature, and Kangol hat turned backward made him look like a little boy playing dress up in his father's suit. "What ya thinking about so hard?" he asked, showing off a gold-crowned smile. "A pretty thing like you should be out there on the floor. You wanna shake a leg with me?"

"Oh, no thank you, sir." I smiled graciously. "I'm not ready to dance just yet. But thanks for the compliments."

"No problem, beautiful. Just do me a favor—keep me in mind when you are ready, because I've got a lot of experience in these old feet."

He called me beautiful. That made me smile hard again. Ever since I lost seventy-four pounds, the looks and compliments had been consistently coming. And even though those compliments made me feel a little bashful, I hadn't gotten tired of hearing them.

Weighing in at 191 pounds, I felt good about myself. I was down to a size fourteen—a size I hadn't seen since the tenth grade—and still losing. But I couldn't take all the credit. I got a lot of help from Ollie. For the last eight months we'd been working out together three to four days a week. It had really been like boot camp, doing weight lifting and cardio techniques she learned from the Army. But when Ollie ran, I speed walked.

I wasn't interested in being super skinny. My goal was to lose forty more pounds and just be healthy and happy. And that's what I learned in my private sessions with Dr. Davenport, a psychologist I met through Rita. Besides letting go of the past and forgiving myself and Uncle Nathan, I needed to lose weight—not so much for looks, but to get healthy so I could have a stronger, more focused mind to handle emotional meltdowns better instead of reaching for Twinkies to alleviate my anxiety and depression.

Now, I wasn't completely happy. There was something still missing in my life. Although my appearance changed and I had more confidence, not one man had asked me out on a proper date yet. But no worries. It was just a matter of time.

The electric slide song came on. Who could resist the electric slide?

"Hey, mister." I tapped the older man's shoulder. "Do you wanna slide?"

Chapter 54

THE first day of March came with a surprise snow shower. But, luckily, it was all melted away and sunny out by Friday. Just in time for the school's annual International Food & Culture Day exhibition on the south lawn. This year I was participating by serving up some free samples of Lowcountry favorites such as shrimp and grits, fried fish, and seafood hush puppies.

My food supply was just about done when Isiah walked up to my table. He was dressed in African attire from head to toe and of course, wearing a wide grin. He took up the small bowl of shrimp and grits to his mouth and then the look of approval formed on his face.

"You like it?" I asked.

"Yes, very much," he said. "The ingredients are simple, but it's very good. Did you make this by yourself?"

"Of course I did." I snickered. "Anyone else would have put sausage, tomatoes, cheese, and Lord knows what else in there. Shrimp and grits is supposed to be simple. Just some onions, spices, and shrimp simmered down into gravy and then poured over creamy grits. That's how Mama taught me."

"Well, after tasting your version, I think your mother is correct."

I gave Isiah a proud smile.

"Listen, I told everyone that I was out of hush puppies, but I saved a few for myself. Would you like to taste one?"

"Yes, please."

He took a bite. Then he closed his eyes and began nodding.

"This is so good. And I like the dash of cayenne pepper. It gives it a kick."

"Thank you, Isiah. I may have to keep you in mind the next time I make them."

Oh my God. Did I just say that?

"Please, do keep me in mind," he agreed. "I would like that."

"So I haven't seen you in a while. What are you doing out here today?" I asked.

"Well, I didn't make a spread like you. Basically, I just handed out information on my country and served Bobotie."

"What's Bobotie?"

"It's like a Southern bread pudding except it's made with a mixture of curried meat and fruit. Bobotie is actually the national dish of my country."

"Okay, and what country are you from?"

"Oh, I'm from South Africa. For some reason I thought you knew that already."

"How would I? I don't know anything about you, just like you know nothing about me."

"That's not all true." He grinned.

"Really?" I said, giving him an amused stare. "What do you think you know about me?"

"Well, for starters, you're a great cook. You're always smiling when I see you around campus, so that means you're nice. And…I think you're beautiful."

"You think I'm beautiful?" I blushed.

"Yes, of course I do."

"Wow, thank you."

Isiah's and my eyes locked. My pulse began to race with excitement. *Is he flirting with me? Don't be silly, Lovely. He's just being friendly.*

"I really need to pack up," I said, breaking our gaze.

"Yes, it's closing time. I should be getting back too. Thanks for the food, Lovely. I'll see you around." Isiah began to leave then stopped. "I hope you don't mind me asking…what are you doing later today?"

Oh my goodness, is he about to ask me out? Play it cool, Lovely.

"Uh, nothing much. I'm just heading home after I clean up. Why?"

"Well, I want to know if you'd like to get a cup of coffee with me. There's a really good coffee shop about two blocks from here. It's just a ten-minute walk."

"You mean today? But I need to change. You do see I have on my uniform?"

"Yes, yes. But who cares?" He shrugged. "Take a look at me. I look like I just stepped away from a photo shoot for *National Geographic* compared to everyone else out here."

We both laughed.

"Trust me," he said, "you look fine."

Chapter 55

LATER that night, I returned home with the biggest smile on my face. You couldn't deflate my cheeks even if they were stuck by pins. It was nearly 10:00 PM. Isiah and I talked all night in the coffee shop until it closed. What a fascinating man he turned out to be. Not only was he an award-winning student, he was also a world traveler and had been all over Africa, the USA, and some European countries. I got so lost in his tales of adventure. He described places I only explored in books. Isiah was, indeed, one cultured, good-looking man. And he was interested in me. We made plans to go out the next night. It would be my first real date.

"Lovely, is that you?" Mama shouted from behind my bedroom door.

"Yes Mama, I'm home." Mama walked in to find me undressing and smiling brightly.

"You're getting home later than usual. Is everything all right?" she asked, wheeling her oxygen tank behind her.

"Yes ma'am, everything's great. I had a late lunch with a friend. That's all."

"You're looking mighty happy."

I nodded. "You know Mama, I am."

She took a seat on my bed and smiled. "Well, are you going to tell me about it?"

I zipped up my housecoat. "I think I've met someone."

"Oh, how wonderful," she said with glee. "With all the hard work you put into losing weight, I just knew you would."

"Yeah, I'm pretty excited too," I added.

"Well, go on. Tell me about him. What's his name?"

"Okay, his name is Isiah Khumalo and—"

"Who?" she interrupted.

"Mama, don't make fun," I whined.

"I'm not, Lovely. Just say his name again and slower this time."

"His name is Isiah Khumalo and he's from South Africa. He's also a fourth-year student at Johnson & Wales."

"Okay, now give me the important stuff, like his age and so and so."

I chuckled inside at Mama's bluntness.

"He's twenty-eight, has no children, his parents are medical professionals and they are all good Christians. So does that meet your approval?"

"I'm not sure, missy. I'll see when he comes over for dinner."

"Whoa, Mama. Don't jump the broom so soon. We haven't even gone on our first date yet."

Mama stood up and coughed. She coughed so hard, the nasal cannula slipped out her left nostril. I reached to adjust it.

"There you go Mama. You're all set."

She smiled. Then took her hand and caressed my face.

"I haven't seen you glow like this in such a long time, child. I don't know what prompted you to lose weight and change your attitude, but I think God for it. You're so much happier now. And that makes you even more beautiful. So you bring that boy over here. I've got a feeling you're really smitten with him."

I could only smile as Mama walked out of my room. As usual, her words were wise and perceptive. She was right, though. Things had changed in my life ever since I got counseling, lost weight, and took on a new way of thinking. It's like I shed my old skin and became something new. And look what I attracted: Isiah.

Chapter 56

"STOP, Ollie!" I yelled. "I can't go any further. I've gotta take a break." I threw my arms over my head and walked around just like Ollie taught me to cool down. It felt like my heart was going to jump out of my chest.

"What's wrong?" Ollie shouted as she jogged back toward me.

"I'm exhausted. That's what's wrong," I gasped, trying to catch my breath.

Ollie stopped in front of me and began jogging in place. "You all right, girl?"

I nodded. "Yeah."

"Good. Because I don't know what made you start running like Flo Jo this morning in the first place. You usually speed walk. It's like you got some burst of energy from somewhere and took off."

I laughed. "Well, I am trying to get it tight, you know. After all, I have a date tonight."

Ollie stopped jogging. "With who?" she exclaimed.

"Isiah Khumalo." I flashed a sassy grin.

"What? Wait? What the hell! When did all of this happen? I just saw you at school yesterday and you didn't say a word."

"I know. It happened so fast. He stopped by my booth yesterday and then asked me to join him for coffee. The next thing I know, we're going on a date tonight."

"Aha! I told you a long time ago that he liked you, remember? And you told me no. Now who's crazy?"

"Yes, yes—you told me. But like my Mama always said, 'Everything in its own time.'"

Ollie teasingly rolled her eyes. "I can't believe you snagged that tall stick of chocolate...yum."

"Wait a minute now," I snapped. "You are talking about my potential man."

She laughed out loud. "Okay, chica. I gotcha. RESPECT."

Slowly, we started walking arm-in-arm down the road.

"You know I'm happy for you." Ollie tugged my arm.

"Yeah, I know."

"And I also know you must be happy that your drought is about to end, because that kitten between your legs has got to be purring for some attention."

I chuckled. "Well, you really can't miss something you've never had."

Ollie shot me a shocked look. "Are saying what I think you're saying? Lovely, are you a virgin?"

"Yep." I nodded my head. "I am a twenty-four-year-old virgin."

"No way, that's impossible."

"Uh, one can survive without sex, Ollie."

"Yeah, but who would want to? Besides, I would get tired of using a vibrator."

I started to laugh. "You could always switch and use your fingers."

"Ha! You would know the tricks of the trade," she said then gave me an odd stare.

"What?"

"Ooh, Isiah is going to tear you up. Or, maybe, you'll turn him out with all those years of wanting and waiting. Either way, you need to make preparations."

"What do you mean?"

"You know—shave your legs, wax your bikini line, get some condoms, and most of all…do some stretches." She laughed.

"Oh, shut up, Ollie. I doubt very much we'll be having sex on the first date."

Ollie's eyes got big. "Hey, you've got no judgment from me. I'm just saying…be prepared."

Chapter 57

I stood in front of my closet trying to find the right outfit. Isiah and I agreed to meet up at Jack's Fun Park to keep the date casual. So I settled on wearing some shape-hugging boot cut jeans and a red V-neck sweater to be comfortable but still appealing.

Before meeting Isiah at the mini-golf course, I stopped by the bathroom to check my hair and face once more. I had never been into makeup in the past, but nowadays I wore eyeliner, mascara, and a little bit of lip gloss almost every day. My weight was down to 185 pounds. And from what I saw in the mirror, I looked damn good.

I walked up behind Isiah and tapped him on the shoulder. "Hello," I said.

"Hello." He greeted me with a big hug. Isiah's embrace was strong and he smelled good too—so good his cologne made me want to sink my teeth into his arm.

Behave, Lovely. Reel it in.

"You look very nice tonight," I said, admiring his physique in dark denim jeans.

He returned the compliment. "I can definitely say the same about you." He looked me over. "I really like your hair. You should wear it down more often."

"Why, thank you."

Isiah put his hand on my back, sending a tingle down my spine. "Come on. Have you ever played Putt Putt before?"

"No, I haven't."

"It's easy. Let me show you how." Isiah hunched his 6'3 frame over my back. I could feel the warmth of his breath on the side of my cheek. Then he took his wide hands and put them over mine. "Now all you have to do is keep your arms straight when you swing the golf club." The little white ball went into the hole. "See," he continued. "Simple, right?"

I wanted to lie to keep Isiah close to me. But I didn't want to appear stupid.

"Yeah, it's simple until the terrain changes."

"Exactly." He nodded. "So are you up for a couple of rounds?"

"Okay, I'm game."

We ended up playing more than two rounds. The design of the volcano-themed course presented a challenge and brought out a competitive spirit in me I hadn't seen since I was a kid. Isiah beat me fair and square by three or four hole-in-ones. But I had fun.

Now we were sitting across from each other in the restaurant Pomodoro Italian sipping on white wine while waiting on our food.

"Do you remember when you started cooking?" Isiah asked.

"Ooh, that's a good question. Yeah, I do remember. I was around eleven years old. I used to watch my mom cook all the time. Then one day, I got in my head to make stew chicken for my parents. And they actually loved it. So I just continued on cooking. What about you?"

"Well, I started cooking later in life. Before culinary school, I worked as a part-time nurse while studying to get into medical school to become a doctor just like my father. But, at the age of twenty-one, a trip to Morocco with some buddies changed my life forever. We stayed in this beautiful riad that was turned into a bed and breakfast."

"Wait. What's a riad?"

"It's a traditional Moroccan house with an inside courtyard in the middle of it."

"Oh, I see. Sorry I interrupted."

"No problem," He grinned. "So the night we arrived, the owners treated us to a welcome dinner in the courtyard. Lovely, I tell you, the curry was so delicious. Those spices danced in my mouth for hours. I charmed my way into the kitchen and got my first cooking lesson that weekend. And after that, I told my father I preferred dissecting chicken instead of human beings."

"You were brave to change your career like that and follow your heart."

"I think so too. I strongly believe you must be happy with what you do in life."

The server returned with our food. I ordered lasagna and Isiah got the Chicken Marsala. We dug in.

"So, Chef Duval, what do you think?" he asked.

I considered the flavors on my tongue. "Honestly, I think we could do better. It's a little too salty for me. What about yours?"

"The sauce is somewhat bland, but edible. Maybe we should skip this place next time."

I grinned. "Yeah, I agree."

Isiah tolerated a few more bites and then began looking at me in a peculiar way.

"What. What is it?" I asked, smiling. "Why are you looking at me like that?"

He chuckled. "How am I looking at you?"

"I don't know. Like you're trying to figure me out or read my thoughts."

"Well, maybe I am," he said, staring at me. "I'm just trying to figure out why you're still single. You're smart and obviously beautiful. I'm actually surprised you're not married yet."

I was flattered. "Well, believe it or not, Isiah. Men do not approach me."

He took a sip of wine then shook his head. "You're right. I don't believe you."

"Oh, it's true. And I'll tell you something else. I don't often date either." I laughed. "Men only started taking notice of me when I lost weight."

"Now that's not true because I noticed you, even when you were heavier."

"Really?"

"Yes," he stressed. "I never understood why most American men idolize skinny women. In my culture, plus-size women are viewed as being beautiful and prosperous."

"So why did it take you this long to say something to me?"

"Honestly, I thought you didn't want to be bothered. The night I met you in the restaurant, you barely looked me in the eyes. That's why I didn't try. It wasn't until recently, when you started smiling and waving at me around campus, I thought— maybe I've got a shot."

I couldn't believe my ears. This whole time I had an admirer and didn't know it. I guess that old saying is true, "You never know who's watching."

I grinned. "Isiah, I am so glad you asked me out, because I know I would have never been bold enough to ask you out first."

"Why?"

Shrugging, I said, "Like I said, I had never been popular with guys in the past."

"Well, in that case, I'm glad I did too."

Isiah and I smiled at each other. We both knew there was something going on between us. For the next hour, we sat in the restaurant and talked until he walked me to my car. And that's when our chemistry became crystal clear. Right there, in the dimly lit parking lot, he kissed me.

Chapter 58

"MAMA, don't forget to put a bay leaf in the soup for me," I said, walking toward the bathroom.

"You don't have to tell me that, child. I've been making okra soup before you were even a thought in Heaven."

I laughed out loud then turned around. "You know I didn't mean any harm. I just want everything to be perfect for tonight."

"I know, Lovely. And it will be…so calm down."

Isiah and I had been going out every weekend for the last three weeks. Mama told me she wouldn't tolerate another weekend of not getting a good look at the man who's been putting a smile on her daughter's face. So I invited Isiah over for dinner and to be examined by her—and no doubt Aunt Harriet too. I gave him fair warning.

I began to fidget with my hair in the mirror. Lately, I'd been trying something new. At night, I'd braid my hair into big sections and then let it loose the next day to get a deep wave look. I'd gotten a lot of compliments on it and Isiah called it sexy.

"How do I look, Mama?" I asked, walking into the kitchen.

"Oh, girl, you look fine. Why are you so nervous?"

"Mama. I've never brought home a guy before, and I really want you to like him. And then…there's Aunt Harriet. I hope she doesn't embarrass me tonight."

"Lovely, I'm sure I'll like Isiah. And don't be worrying about Harriet. She's got a lot of mouth, but she's harmless."

The screen door slammed shut.

"It's getting dark out. And y'all need to lock this front door," Aunt Harriet hollered. "Times are different now. You just can't leave the door open like we used to around here."

Oh Lord, here she comes. "Mama, please keep her in line," I whispered.

Aunt Harriet stood in the kitchen with her hands on her hip. "So where's this African boy I'm supposed to meet? Because I'm hungry."

"He'll be here any minute," I said.

Aunt Harriet took a seat. "Who curled your hair, Dolores? It looks nice."

"Thank you. Lovely curled it for me."

"Well, ain't nobody told me I was supposed to get dressed up."

"You're fine, Aunt Harriet."

"Aha," she mumbled. "What's on the menu?"

"We've got okra soup, white rice, baked pork chops and cornbread," Mama said.

"Good," Aunt Harriet replied. "I was afraid Lovely was going to cook that fancy stuff she learned at that school."

I chuckled. "No, Aunt Harriet. I want Isiah to taste a typical Southern home-cooked meal."

There was a knock at the door. I looked at Mama excitedly. "That's him!" I scurried through the living room to open the door. And there stood my fine boyfriend in the doorway. I welcomed Isiah with an enthusiastic smile and kiss.

"How are you?" I asked.

"I'm good," he said, rubbing my arms.

"Did you have any trouble finding us out here?"

"No. Not at all."

"Good," I said then looked behind me. "Are you ready?"

He flashed a confident grin. "Yes. Why not?"

We walked into the kitchen holding hands. "Mama, Aunt Harriet, this is Isiah Khumalo."

"Hello, it is very nice to meet you both," he said.

"Hello, Isiah," Mama said.

"Hello, young man," said Aunt Harriet.

"Ah, I heard you two like chocolate covered cherries, so I brought some along."

Aunt Harriet gasped. "Oh, a good-looking man who brings chocolate. He's a keeper, Lovely."

Isiah put the box on the table and took a seat while I started serving dinner.

"So, Isiah. Lovely tells me you will be receiving your bachelor's degree in culinary arts this coming May. Are you excited? Mama asked.

"Yes, ma'am. It's been a long four years, but enjoyable."

"You've been here in America for only four years?" Aunt Harriet blurted out. "And your English is that good?"

Isiah laughed. But I rolled my eyes while I slapped food on plates.

"I went to a private school so I learned English at an early age. However, there are a lot of South Africans who speak English."

"Really," Aunt Harriet said. "Now that's interesting."

"Isiah, do you plan on staying here in the United States after graduation or will you be returning home?" Mama asked.

"I actually plan on making the U.S. my home."

Mama liked his answer. I saw the smile on her face as I walked up to the table. "Here's dinner," I said, setting down plates. "I hope you like okra soup, Isiah."

"Of course I do," he declared. In my culture, men say, 'A woman who can cook a proper okra soup is a woman worth marrying.'"

"I heard that." Aunt Harriet chuckled.

We all joined hands and then Mama blessed the food.

"Now, I want you to tell me the truth about my soup, Isiah." I winked.

Isiah scooped up the chunky soup into his mouth. He closed his eyes and then a pleased expression appeared on his face.

"I guess that means you like it."

"Oh, yes indeed."

"So tell me something, Isiah. Is it true African men can have multiple wives at the same time?" Aunt Harriet asked.

I shook my head. *Why try?*

After dinner, I walked Isiah to his car. He leaned back on the door of his silver Toyota Camry and gazed up at the night sky. The weather was nice and the stars were out. He smiled.

"Why are you smiling?" I asked. "What do you see?"

Isiah sighed. "The stars and the seclusion out here just remind me of my grandfather's small farm back at home. It's peaceful."

"Do you miss Africa?" I asked.

"Yes, sometimes."

"My sister, Irene, the one I told you that died…she really wanted to go to Africa. In fact she was going to teach there. I wonder…do you think I would like Africa?"

"Absolutely, the way you like food and diversity—you'd fit right in."

I nodded.

"Listen, I am so sorry about my Aunt Harriet and her stupid questions tonight."

"Aw, she didn't bother me. I enjoyed your family. Besides, there are a lot of people in this country who think Africans live in huts and wear loincloths all day."

I snickered. "But you know they can't help their ignorance. Most people only know what they see on television."

"You're right," he said, pulling me into his waist. "And aren't I lucky you weren't one of them." Isiah gazed into my eyes intensely. "I want to do something nice for you since you did something nice for me."

"Okay. And what is that, sir?" I asked, intrigued.

"Let me cook dinner for you at my place. We'll spend a quiet evening all alone. How does that sound?"

Like I would say no to a romantic dinner! "Sounds good."

Later that night, I lay in bed thinking about Irene again. I remembered how badly she wanted to live in Africa but fate intervened. Now Africa was at my doorstep. I couldn't help but wonder…was this just serendipity or God's way of mending a broken dream?

Chapter 59

I knew Isiah lived with his older cousin. That's why he chose to study in South Carolina. But I didn't know his cousin lived like a king in a posh condo just minutes away from the beach in Mt. Pleasant.

"What did you say Lwazi does for a living?" I asked.

"Oh, he's a dentist," Isiah said, still cooking. "But if you give me a few minutes, I'll give you a tour."

"No problem," I said, turning around on the bar stool to get another scan of the open concept living room and kitchen. The décor in the living room was elegant and modern with accents of African art. The kitchen was just as impressive with updated appliances and dark wood cabinets. All of it was masculine and very clean. But the focal point of the condo had to be the view from the long balcony.

"Y'all have a fantastic view of the harbor," I said.

"I know," he agreed. He pointed toward the balcony. "If you go outside, you can see downtown Charleston. And if you think that's impressive, you should see the sunsets here. They're just amazing."

"Wow. Dentistry is really treating Lwazi well. I'm surprised no woman has him on lock."

"Lwazi get married? I don't think so. He's enjoying his bachelor's life way too much to settle down. Not even his mother can do that."

"So, how old is he?"

"Ah…Lwazi is thirty-three."

"Oh-my-goodness, Isiah. That's still young. He has time."

"Not according to his mother." He snickered. "She wants her grandchildren now."

"So where is he tonight? I'd like to meet him."

"He's actually out of town attending a conference this weekend. But I definitely want you to meet him too."

"You *definitely* want me to meet him?" I asked, smiling big.

"Of course I do. You're very important to me." Isiah returned a smile then suddenly started coughing.

"Oh, not you too." I frowned. "Are you all right?"

Isiah turned the stove off then got a cup of water to drink. "I'm fine." He coughed one last time. "Just got some pepper fumes into my lungs." He poured two glasses of white wine. "What did you mean, a second ago, when you said, 'Not you too?'"

I let out a sigh. "I was just talking about Mama. She's been coughing so much lately. I'm beginning to think her heart condition is slowly getting worse. I almost canceled our date tonight because I didn't want to leave her alone."

Isiah set his down glass and began massaging my shoulders. "Lovely, you do a lot for your mother. I'm sure she's fine. Besides, you deserve a break. And I know your mother would agree."

He stopped massaging my arms. "I know what will cheer you up." He went to the entertainment stand and pulled out a CD. Isiah looked back at me with a grin. "This is my favorite singer in the whole world."

A Latin rhythm began to sway my shoulders. It was Stevie Wonder's "Don't You Worry 'Bout A Thing" playing. The room was filled with uplifting music and the smell of exotic spices. Isiah extended his hands for a dance. I couldn't help but smile and give in.

Closely, we moved to the beat, laughing while we made up salsa moves. Then he spun me around and around until, finally, our eyes locked and our laughter faded into serious stares. He cupped my chin and lifted my face. "I love you," he said, "and as long as I'm in your life, you don't have to worry about anything."

Isiah's words seemed sincere. I felt safe. And just like that, a surge of heat ran wild through my body, and I became wet. I couldn't fight it any longer.

"I'm ready," I said, barely able to speak.

"Are you sure?" he asked.

My arousal was so intense all I could do was nod and pant softly.

In the bedroom, I nervously stood before Isiah in a towel. He was naked. His body was tight and muscular and his penis—more than ample. "I know this is your first time so I'll be gentle," he whispered. "Don't be afraid of me."

I looked away.

"What's wrong?" he asked.

"I really want to be with you, but I'm ashamed to show you my body. I'm still fat."

Isiah turned my face. "I don't see a fat woman. I only see a beautiful woman. So, please, don't project your insecurities onto me." He took his hands and ran them down my sides, feeling my fat rolls through the towel. "You see, to me, these small mounds you call fat are just speed bumps I will gladly take my time crossing with my lips."

"You really don't mind?"

"No. Will you let me show you?"

In that reassuring moment, I decided to drop my towel and fear to lie on my back and spread wide for Isiah. And as promised, he kissed me everywhere, making it easier for him to push inside me inch by inch. The quick stinging pressure of losing my virginity soon became pleasure.

"Please," I begged and moaned while clutching his back. In response he pumped harder and faster. Then finally, with my eyes closed and mouth open, the tension mounting within me exploded. Isiah freed me.

Chapter 60

WAKING up in the arms of a man was something else I had never experienced before. Isiah's hard body spooning mine made me feel desired and secure. I don't know how I found strength to leave his protection to return home to Mama.

Now I lay in my own bed, basking in the early morning sunlight—enjoying my recent rise in womanhood. I felt good and relaxed. And although my thighs and vagina were a little sore, I reveled in it. Just like I reveled in the fact that I could still smell Isiah's cologne engulfing my entire body. That man had me feeling brand new and finally…grown.

"Lovely," Mama said, from the hallway.

"Yes, ma'am," I answered quickly. Her voice, now fragile, still carried a lot of authority.

"Come on out of that bedroom. Breakfast is ready."

I sprung up and into my robe. "Good morning, Mama," I said, walking to the kitchen with a gigantic smile on my face. "You didn't have to make breakfast. I could have done this."

"Well, I didn't want to wake you up since you came home so late."

"You heard me come in? I thought you were asleep."

Mama snickered as she sat down to eat. "Didn't I tell you before, child? I know about everything that goes on in my house."

"I guess you do, Mama."

"How was your date last night?" she asked, grinning.

"It was good," I replied, trying hard to conceal my excitement.

"Just good?" Mama chuckled. "I'd say it was more than good. I know that look on your face, missy. I see your wild hair. Your father used to make me look like that too."

"Mama, be nice."

"I am being nice," she teased. "I just think you had relations with that young man last night. Now tell me I'm wrong."

Mama saw straight through me like an x-ray machine. There was no point in lying.

"Are you disappointed?" I asked.

"No, hun," she said warmly. "Now I have to admit, I wish you would have waited for your wedding night. But I understand these are different times. Besides, I suppose you waited long enough. And you do have a good head on your shoulders. So I trust you chose the right man to take your virginity."

"Oh, Mama, I did. I'm in love," I said gleefully. "And for the first time in my life, I'm loved back. And that's why I'm so glad you really like him because he may be the one."

Mama chuckled again.

"Why are you laughing?" I asked.

"Child, it's just that sparkle in your eye reminds me of the night I fell in love with your father at the county fair." She chuckled once more. "And it almost didn't happen."

She piqued my curiosity. "Why is that?"

"Well, you see, Joseph Duval was a pretty boy in his youth and he knew it. Ooh, Lovely, you should've seen your father back then. He had light brown eyes and wavy soft hair that made the girls go crazy. So when he approached me at a diner, I already knew about his reputation and played hard to get. Now I was able to brush him off for about two weeks. But, eventually, his persistence broke me down and we started courting. And then finally, on a Ferris wheel, he gave me a promise ring—making it clear to everyone that I was his one and only girl. That's when I knew he was the one."

"Mama, that sounded so magical."

"It was baby. And now I am so glad you've found some magic and happiness of your own after all these years. I never doubted for a second that God would put love in your life." Mama raised her hand to her mouth and started coughing.

"Are you all right?"

"Yes, I'm fine," she said, taking a sip of tea. "It's just my sinuses are getting the best of me this morning."

Mama blew her nose and cleared her throat once again.

"So you think you're in love," she continued. "Tell me how that feels for you."

"Oh, Mama, it's like nothing on earth can go wrong as long as I can hear Isiah's voice and see his face. He just feels like home. "

"Yep, you're in love. But just remember two things. Number one—there will be no sleepovers in my house. And secondly, if Isiah wants your loving on the regular, you make him give you a commitment, because my daughter is no cheap thrill."

I smiled hard. "Yes, ma'am."

Chapter 61

May 1998

GRADUATION day came and went in a flash. Mama and I got the chance to meet Isiah's parents, and that went better than expected. For some reason, I had it in my head they would have a problem with me not being from Africa. But I was more than wrong.

The Khumalos embraced me with so much warmth. "So you're the woman who's making my son so very happy," Mrs. Khumalo told me with a hug. "You should know Isiah speaks very highly of you whenever he calls home." After several more hugs that day, she gave me an invitation to visit South Africa and meet the rest of the family. I happily accepted.

When everything went back to normal, Isiah treated me to a weekend getaway to Myrtle Beach, SC. We slummed on the beach, frolicked in the water, and made love every night to the sound of crashing waves. The trip was exactly what I needed: relaxation, romance, and complete avoidance of responsibility and seeking employment. Now I was staring at Ollie with a blank face in my den.

"No, I don't have a new job lined up," I said to answer her question.

"I guess not." She snickered. "You've been too busy being underneath Isiah these last couple of months to even think about life after graduation."

"Guilty as charged," I admitted, grinning.

"And what happened to us working out together? We haven't done that in weeks."

I sucked my teeth. "Ollie, let me have fun."

"Oh, I want you to have fun. Just don't neglect me and our workouts. Tell me something. How much do you weigh?"

"Uhg," I groaned. "Really, Ollie?"

"Yes, really...how much do you weigh?"

I shrugged. "I don't know. Last week I weighed 192 pounds."

"192 pounds!" Ollie exclaimed. "You've gained seven pounds."

"Girl, calm down. It's just seven pounds. Besides, Isiah doesn't care."

"Trust me. Seven pounds can turn into twenty pounds just like that." She snapped her fingers. "And another thing, you weren't losing weight for a man. You were working out for your health."

"Yes, Ollie—I know. You're right, and I'll get back on the wagon soon."

"Good." She twisted her lips.

"So when do you start your fancy job at the Charleston Place Inn?" I asked.

"In two weeks. And I am so excited. I can't believe I'm going to be the assistant pastry chef. Hey, what about Isiah?"

"You know, I'm not sure. I know he applied to several restaurants. And I know he mentioned something about doing another advanced program at Johnson & Wales. But that's all he's told me."

I looked at Mia sitting on the floor playing with cookies she no longer seemed interested in. "Are you done with your cookies and milk, sweetheart?"

"Yes, ma'am," she replied.

I scooped up her dishes and headed for the kitchen. Then suddenly my mind went back on Ollie's question about my weight. *How much do I weigh?* I made a detour for the bathroom and stood on the scale. It read 198. Yeah, I was not going to tell drill sergeant Ollie about that one.

Chapter 62

"HOW do you do it?" Isiah asked while sweeping strands of hair away from my face.

"How do I do what?" I smiled.

"Look so beautiful when you wake up. I could watch you sleep for hours."

"Well, sir, I heard someone say on an old black and white movie that a woman is only beautiful when she's been truly loved."

"So that explains everything," he said, hovering over my body. Then he leaned in for a kiss. "What are you in the mood for—a full Southern breakfast or just some mango and cheese?"

"Hmm, let me think. Mango and cheese, please."

He kissed me again. "Your wish is my command, my queen. I'll be right back."

Isiah walked away wearing the black silk boxers I bought for his birthday a few weeks ago. He looked just as sexy as the night he first put them on to give me a strip tease. And that's where we were in our relationship. Not only did we have good verbal intimacy, we were absolutely comfortable sharing and playing out our wildest sexual fantasies. Just last night, I wore some red stiletto heels in bed. It drove Isiah insane. And of course, the sex was hot.

Isiah returned to the room grinning with a food tray in his hands. I sat up against the headboard. "You look extremely happy. What's up?"

He put the tray on my lap and then fed me a slice of mango. "I'm glad you asked. Look what came for me in the mail," he said, holding a letter.

"Okay. Don't keep me in suspense. Who's it from?"

"It's from Le Cuisine. Lovely, they're offering me a job!"

"You mean Le Cuisine in New York City? The French restaurant with three Michelin stars?"

"Yes. Yes. I'm so excited! This is fantastic news!"

I was happy for Isiah, but he never told me about the possibility of him moving to New York. "Congratulations. I'm so happy for you."

"You are? But you're not smiling, my love."

"Well, I guess because I'm also shocked. You never told me that you applied for a job out of state."

"I know, Lovely," he said, putting the tray on the dresser. "I didn't want to mention it because I wasn't too confident I would get it. When the executive chef came to teach a class, I assisted him. He liked my technique and told me I should send him my resume. So I did. But their entry-level positions are so competitive, I didn't think much of it."

"I understand all of that," I said. "But you could have given me a heads up. I thought we were telling each other everything?"

"We *do* tell each other everything. But I really thought this job would be such a long shot, it wasn't even worth talking about."

"So now what?" I asked.

"What do you mean…now what?"

"I mean, what are you going to do?"

"Lovely, this is an opportunity of a lifetime. I must go."

"For how long?"

"Lovely, it's a job. Maybe a year or two."

"One or two years?" I snapped then got out of bed to put on my clothes.

"Lovely, I don't understand. Why are you so upset?"

"Why am I upset? Isiah, what about us? Have you even thought about that?"

"Yes, I have," he stressed. "Listen, why don't you move with me?"

I rolled my eyes. "Really, Isiah, how do you suppose I do that when I have a sick mother to take care of?"

"Okay. But we still make this work. You could always visit me, right?"

"You know I'm not comfortable being far away from Mama too long."

"Well, I'll just come back here when I can."

"How realistic is that? You're going to be working crazy hours almost every day."

Isiah sat on the edge of the bed. He knew I was right. We had obligations.

"So what do you want me to do? Give up my job? Give up my dreams of making a name for myself in the culinary world? Lovely, Le Cuisine is going to give me the chance to prove to my family that I can make some real money doing what I love instead of practicing medicine."

I picked up my overnight bag and purse. "Isiah, I don't want you to give up anything because I'm not going to be labeled the selfish girlfriend who blocked your dreams. I am truly, truly happy for you. And I want you to succeed. So follow your heart and go to New York. Make a name for yourself."

In the house, I put up a brave front. But in the car I cried knowing I did the right thing by letting Isiah go. A long distance relationship would have never worked for me. I craved his attention and love too much. And asking him to stay would only cause resentment toward me down the line. Clearly, this was our fork in the road. He had his priorities and so did I.

Chapter 63

"ARE you done yet?" Ollie sarcastically asked.

"Nope, I'm just getting started," I replied, squeezing a packet of mayonnaise on a double bacon cheeseburger. A disgusted frown washed over Ollie's face.

"So you're going to sit there and eat that hamburger on top of those fries and large milkshake you just sucked down?"

I nodded. "Yep, that's the plan."

Ollie folded her arms over. I knew she was upset with me. Her squinted gaze and bouncing crossed leg told the whole story.

"Listen, Ollie, I told you I didn't feel like coming out. I told you I was going through something. But, being the bossy person you are, you insisted I come meet you at the mall today. So this is what you get...me in raw form."

Ollie snickered contemptuously, and leaned forward. "I'm going to let that bossy remark slide because I know you're hurting. After all, I'm just a friend who cares. But Lovely, you've been moping for nearly two weeks and by the looks of it, probably binge eating as well."

I shrugged then bit into the burger. "Like you said, I'm hurting—right?"

"Listen, chica," Ollie said. "Do you think you're the only woman who's been hurt or let down by a man? Hell no! You're not the first and you're damn sure not going to be the last. I get it. Isiah was your first love. But there will be other loves. And—"

"Stop talking at me like I'm a child, Ollie," I snapped. "I may not have had many boyfriends, but I understand loss and disappointments more than you know. It's just...I waited a very long time for love. It took so long to find someone I could trust and feel safe to take care of my needs. See, you don't know what it's like to wait year after year for something as simple as attention and human contact. I've been through a lot, Ollie. And I've done a lot of good for other people. I just thought God would let me have this one thing in my life."

Ollie sighed. "I didn't mean to sound condescending," she said softly. "And you're right. I have no clue what it's like to wait so long for love. I've always had boyfriends. I'm just saying love can sometimes suck. But, you've got to keep it moving." She stood up. "Look, Lovely, I'm going to go. I just can't sit here and watch you eat yourself into a diabetic coma. I can't watch you destroy all the hard work you put into losing weight."

My eyes started to water. "Wait. Don't go. I'm not as strong as you, Ollie."

"Yes you are, Lovely!" Ollie sat back down and pushed the food tray away. "Before Mia came into the picture, Marcos sold me dreams of us getting married and raising a family. But when I got pregnant, he ran for the hills—leaving me to raise our daughter alone. I was so devastated and felt abandoned. And yes, at first, I didn't think I was strong enough either. But when my child was placed in my arms, I knew I had no choice because I loved her. And you know what...I loved me too."

Ollie touched my hand. "This is what I had to ask myself: Should I allow Marcos to make me go into a deep depression and look bad while he lived it up? Hell no! Trust me—staying fly and happy is the best revenge. Do you know how many times he's tried to get back with me? Too damn many."

I dried my face with a napkin. "Ollie, I need help."

"I know you do, sweetie. And the first thing we're going to do is get out of this food court and go for a walk."

Chapter 64

I walked in the house to hear the phone ringing. The caller ID said it was Mrs. Hall, formally Ms. Gwen Turner. I was surprised to see the call, especially since I hadn't heard much from her since she married Gerald and moved away from Willisburg four years ago.

"Hello Mrs. Hall. How are you?" I asked, pulling off my work hair net. "He's where? He's got what?"

***

Walking down the long corridor at MUSC in what the nurse called infection control garments, I felt a heavy since of dread anticipating what I was about to see. I knew about AIDS. I saw the public service announcements on television and read articles about it in office lobbies.

But now I knew someone personally with the horrible disease.

I stood in front of the door and took a deep breath behind my mask. Then with my trembling hand, I turned the knob and pushed the door in to see a friend I hadn't seen in seven years.

"Jamal," I gasped with watering eyes.

He was thin. His head was bald and there were IV lines and other wires connected to him. He lifted his eyes from a magazine and gave me a shocked stare. His eyes were the only thing I saw because his mouth was covered with a white mask.

"Child, don't you come in here with those crocodile tears. Ain't nobody dying today. I'll be out of this hospital bed within a week—you'll see."

Jamal coughed and then pointed to the windowsill. "Hand me that box of tissue, please." He lowered his mask and wiped his mouth. "Can you believe a simple thing such as the common cold has put my ass back in the hospital? The doctor told me since my immune system is suppressed, it's easier for me to catch an infection and harder to get rid of it. That's why we're both wearing these irritating masks. But you probably already knew that. Didn't you, smarty-pants?" Jamal chuckled then placed the magazine on the nightstand. "Lovely, don't just stand there. Have a seat."

I pulled a chair close to his bedside and sat.

"You look good, girl," he said. You've slimmed down and your hair looks so nice."

"Thank you."

"Did my mother tell you about me?" he asked.

I nodded. "Yes."

"I told that woman not to worry your nerves." Jamal shook his head. "I didn't want you to see me this way."

"Why didn't you tell me?"

He shrugged. "I guess I didn't know how to tell you."

"How long have you known?"

"About a year. I found out when I tried to sell my blood." He snickered. "Imagine my surprise."

"How are you feeling?"

"Well, I have my good days and then my bad. Today is a good day." Jamal reached for my gloved hand. "I'm so glad to see you, Lovely."

I closed my eyes and let the tears fall. I couldn't help it. "You can beat this thing. If anyone can do it, it's you, Jamal. Besides, people are living longer with HIV and AIDS today. Look at Magic Johnson."

"Oh, honey, don't cry for me. I know this shit is going to kill me—maybe not now, but one day."

"Don't talk like that," I snapped.

"Lovely, I don't have the money for fancy medicines or good health insurance. All I can do is hope for the best, but I've already prepared myself for the worst."

"Jamal, I have a little money saved up. Whatever you need, you know it's yours. I just want you to fight."

"And that's what I'll continue to do. But, listen Lovely, this is in God's hands. So whatever happens…happens. Okay?"

I nodded. "I just want you to know that I love you."

"I know. And I love you too, sis. Now go on over there and wash your hands so you can wipe your eyes. I told you all the crying wasn't necessary."

"Be quiet, Jamal," I said, moving toward the sink.

"Look at Miss Lovely in those jeans. So who's the man responsible for your new shape? And don't be telling me you're still a virgin because that would be a damn lie."

I chuckled. "His name was Isiah."

"What do you mean his name…*was*? Is the man dead?"

I shook my head. "No, silly. We broke up a few months ago."

"Why, girl?"

"He found a job in New York City."

"New York City. Shit. You should of gone with him."

"And leave Mama? I don't think so."

"There you go, still putting the weight of the world on your shoulders. Well, was he at least good in bed?"

I smiled so hard my eyes narrowed into slits.

"I guess that's a yes," he said. "I can see your toothy grin behind that mask. He was your first piece, wasn't he?"

"Yes, he was my first," I answered sweetly.

"Okay, miss thing, get me caught up. How was your first time?"

"Well, it did sting a little in the beginning, but I got over that quick."

"I guess it did sting—as long as you had your legs closed. I bet that man had to use a crowbar to open that hole."

I busted out into loud laughter and then Jamal joined right in. It was like old times.

Chapter 65

I found myself a stranger in a familiar place this morning. I hadn't been a regular at Mt. Moriah Baptist church since I entered cooking school. Even Mama's attendance had been scarce since she grew sick. But Aunt Harriet kept our long-standing spot on the third row bench secured with her nearly perfect attendance record.

I made a lot of heads turn the moment I stepped into the building. Whispers abounded when I walked down the aisle—typical for the gossipers in Mt. Moriah church. As I scooted past knees to find a seat, some old timers sitting in my row gave me glowing compliments on my appearance. That's when I realized people were mostly staring at me because of my weight loss rather than my return.

I had an alternative motive for showing up in church. Not only had I gone to pray for the health and strength of Mama and Jamal, I specifically went to see Anika. The church celebrated its seventy-third anniversary today and Anika performed. And of course, she brought the house down with her anointed voice.

Aunt Harriet and I didn't stay long after lunch. I wanted to get back home to check on Mama. Last night, she had a rare asthma attack and it took me the longest time to find her inhaler. Although the attack was mild, it scared me senseless and made me not want to leave her side. But Mama insisted I go to church. And I'm glad I did. It was nice to meet Anika's new baby girl and catch up on our lives.

During the drive home, Aunt Harriet just couldn't wait to eat her takeaway in her own house. The second after she fastened the seatbelt, she began picking at a huge chunk of cornbread wrapped up in wax paper. Crumbs were all over her dress and fingers.

"Aunt Harriet, do you need a napkin?" I asked. "There should be some in the glove compartment."

"No, I think I'll be all right," she replied, wiping her hand on the bottom of her dress.

I couldn't believe she was still eating. I know I saw her eat a full plate before we left. That was the peculiar thing about Aunt Harriet. At the age of seventy-five, she ate everything: popcorn, hamburgers, fries, honeybuns, etc. But she didn't have high cholesterol or diabetes.

"Church service was good today. Wasn't it, Lovely?" Aunt Harriet asked.

"Yes, ma'am, it was."

"Anika sounded wonderful as usual. And did you get a look at her baby? What a beautiful little girl. I remember when Anika was just a short stack singing her heart out on the stage and now she has a baby of her own. I tell ya time sure does fly." Aunt Harriet gave me a light slap on my thigh. "Soon you'll be pushing out a little one too."

I flashed a smile.

"So when is Isiah returning from New York?" she asked.

The question caught me off guard. Just like I never had the heart to tell Aunt Harriet and Mama about Jamal's HIV status, I never told them that Isiah and I actually broke up, only that he got a job out of state. But I knew Mama got the hint when the phone calls from Isiah stopped. "I'm not sure. I think Isiah is going to be there for a while."

"Oh, I see," she said, breaking off another piece of cornbread. "Wasn't it nice how Pastor Holmes spoke so highly about Dolores and asked everyone to pray for her return?" she continued. "What did he call her? 'A faithful matron of the church who's never complained.' Oh, I've gotta to tell her about the love she received today and all the people who miss her so much."

"Yes, you must," I agreed. "But did you know they were going to call me up to accept her lifetime service award?"

"Yes, I did. I was going to do it, but I knew you were coming. Was there a problem?"

"Oh, no. I'm just not very comfortable standing up in front of an audience."

"I don't know why. Mt. Moriah is your home. You know those people. And you look so pretty standing up there. As a matter of fact, several people asked me why you haven't been coming to church."

And there it was. A conversation I really didn't want to have with Aunt Harriet. We had different views on religion. I believed in God, even though sometimes I felt God had forgotten me—I was no atheist. But I didn't believe a person had to go to church every single Sunday to be a good Christian. And I definitely didn't believe all Christians in the church were good. Mt. Moriah taught me that lesson at a young age when mean-spirited members used to spread nasty rumors in church. That's why, a long time ago, I chose to place my faith in God, not a building and its occupants.

"I've got to work and take care of Mama," I said, hoping a short answer would suffice.

"And that's what I told them," she said. "There's nothing more Christian than taking care of your mother. Trust me...the Lord will bless you for it."

I nodded, grateful my comment didn't strike up a debate on religious philosophies. The last heated exchange we had was over Jamal's sexual orientation and how she felt he was condemning himself to Hell. These days, she seemed less combative. Instead of standing on a soapbox, Aunt Harriet just continued to eat and talk about random things. And by the time we got home, that takeout box was almost empty.

Chapter 66

IT was a beautiful August day. The weather couldn't have been better for gardening. Mama and Aunt Harriet were sitting in rocking chairs on the porch flipping through an old photo album while I worked in the flowerbeds.

The color purple seemed to be the theme for this season. I planted all sorts of colorful wild flowers around the yard last spring—marigolds, sunflowers, and daisies just to name a few. But the purple lupines and cornflowers shot up lush and brilliant in color—outshining the rest. Even the African violets Mama placed next to the front door seemed more vibrant this year.

A warm gentle breeze and laughter from Mama and Aunt Harriet brought back a pleasant memory from my childhood. I looked across the street at the field. It was like I could see me and Jamal laughing and flying kites. I closed my eyes and said a silent prayer for my friend. It had been almost a month since I heard from him. About two weeks after leaving the hospital, he left town. Not even his mother knew where he went.

Aunt Harriet's loud outburst grabbed my attention.

"What are you two cackling about?" I asked.

"Oh, we're just laughing at this picture," Aunt Harriet said.

"What about it?" I asked, walking up the steps with a grin.

She handed me an old black and white photograph. "That's a picture of your uncle Richard with a relaxer in his hair. Back then, black men used to perm their hair to make it look smooth and slick like white folks. But do you see his bugged out eyes?" Aunt Harriet started laughing again. "I told that fool that lye was going to burn his scalp if he left it in too long. I am so glad I had a camera nearby to capture that moment."

"Those were some good times," Mama said, turning a page. "Oh, my heavens. Harriet, do you remember these red and white polka dot dresses?"

"Of course I do," Aunt Harriet said proudly. "I'm the one who made those matching Easter dresses for you and Irene. Hands down, Irene was the prettiest little girl in church that morning."

"And look at this one, Harriet. It's a picture of Joseph at Addie's elementary school graduation. Oh, he looked so handsome that day."

Mama sighed. "Lord knows I miss my babies. There's not a day that goes by that I don't think about him or Irene."

Mama gave me a soft smile and then looked out at the yard.

"The flowers and the vegetables sure did come up good this summer. You did a beautiful job again, Lovely. I don't think there's anything else I can teach you about gardening."

"I'm no horticulturist. But I think I do all right."

"Oh, I think you do more than all right," she said, grabbing her cane. "Help me to my bedroom, Lovely. I'm feeling a little tired."

I removed Mama's blanket and then lifted her thin, frail body. Slowly we walked to her bed.

"Do you want your oxygen?" I asked, getting her comfortable.

"No, I don't want to wear that silly thing right now. I'll be fine," she said, sounding exhausted.

"Well, there you are, Mama—all tucked in. Is there anything else I can do for you?"

"No, sweetheart. You've done enough." She reached for my hand. "Lovely, I want to thank you for everything you've done."

"Mama, you don't have to thank me. I should be thanking you." I smiled.

"Just listen to me, baby girl. I know life hasn't always been easy for you. I've watched you sacrifice a lot of your young years to take care of me and your father without one complaint. You're truly a fine woman with a good heart. And that's why I thank God for you. You must know it's been a privilege being your mother."

"Mama, why are you talking like this? I know how much you love me."

"Yes, but tomorrow isn't promised to anyone. That's why it's important to say things now—while you can."

I chuckled, not taking Mama's comment seriously. "Okay, in that case, I want to thank you for being the most loving and understanding mother in the world. I don't know what I'd do without you." I smiled then kissed her forehead.

Mama yawned. "You don't need me anymore, baby girl," she said in a whisper as her heavy eyelids began to drift closed.

"You're doing fine. Just keep the faith. And remember—God has many blessings in store for you."

I let go of Mama's hand when I heard a light snore.

"I love you, Mama. I'll wake you up for dinner."

***

"Did these yellow squash come from the garden today?" Aunt Harriet asked, hovering over my pan of sautéed squash with onions and bacon.

"Yes, they did," I replied.

"Well they look pretty—almost too pretty to eat."

"I know. Must be the new fertilizer I used," I said, taking off my apron. "Let me get Mama up for dinner."

I went into the bedroom and flipped on the lights. "Mama, it's time for dinner," I said, walking toward her.

She didn't respond. Her face and body appeared absolutely still.

"MAMA!"

Chapter 67

MAMA died from natural causes in her sleep. The medical examiner said her heart just simply stopped. Knowing she went peacefully and didn't suffer in the end helped me sleep at night, but it didn't diminish the pain. I missed her too much.

As Mama requested, we buried her in a plot next to Daddy and Irene in a cemetery across the street from Mt. Moriah Baptist church. The burial site was flooded with people. Some said it was the largest funeral they had ever attended. As we dispersed from the grounds, a familiar face in the distance caught my attention. It was a sharply dressed black woman with glasses and long hair standing underneath a tree. I knew who she was the moment our eyes locked. It was that mysterious woman I met several years ago back at the grocery store where I worked.

I looked back and shouted to Cynthia, "Go on to the repass without me. I'll be there in a few minutes." I don't know why, but I felt compelled to confront the woman. When I started walking toward her, she quickly walked off.

"Excuse me, ma'am!" I shouted. But the woman kept on walking. "Excuse me!" I shouted again. Then she finally stopped.

"I remember you," I said. "You're the woman from the grocery store."

She turned around. "Yes, Lovely, I am."

The way the woman looked at me and knowingly said my name triggered my suspicion.

"Who are you—really?" I asked.

The woman took off her glasses and then let out a breath. "I really didn't want us to meet like this, but my name is Corinne Scott. Lovely…I'm your mother."

Like a deer in the headlights, I couldn't move anything— especially my lips. But I could see. Scanning her up and down with an eagle's eye, I noticed we shared the same shape, the same hair texture, and the same milk chocolate skin. I knew she was telling the truth. Her facial features were etched on my face. She looked nothing like her yearbook picture. She wore glasses now. And that's why I didn't recognize her long ago.

"Listen, I know you're in shock and have nothing to say," she said. "I realize this was not the best time to make myself known. But I couldn't stay away from Mrs. Duval's funeral. I just couldn't—she meant so much to me."

I heard Corinne's words but they sounded muffled as my brain tried to process her sudden appearance.

"Like I said, I'm sure this is a lot for you to digest right now. But I'm hoping, when everything settles down, we could get together to talk. I have so much to tell you."

I still had no words for my birth mother. Feeling blindsided, all I could do was stare. She took a pen out of her purse and then began writing on the funeral's program. "Here's my cell phone number. If you want to meet, just let me know."

Still stunned, I took Corinne's number and watched her walk off. To me, the shock of seeing Corinne was just as shocking as if I had seen Mama's ghost.

Chapter 68

CYNTHIA was not having it. As far as she was concerned, Harriet Tillman was her only mother. And there was no reason to meet Corinne. I, on the other hand, always had a lingering curiosity about her. Besides, I learned in therapy that forgiveness is not so much for those who do you wrong, but for the victim's peace of mind and salvation.

It took three weeks for that wisdom to cement into my soul and schedule a place and time to meet up with Corinne. We settled on one afternoon at Hampton Park. And there I was sitting at a picnic table underneath a large Willow Oak tree face to face with my birthmother. I always thought I'd have a flood of questions the moment we met. But I just sat there limited to cordial words.

"It's shaping up to be a beautiful September day, isn't it?" Corinne asked, opening the conversation.

"Yes, it is." I flashed a smile. "The temperature is perfect."

Corinne returned the smile then took off her glasses. She was attractive and looked youthful with only a touch of makeup on her well-preserved face. But the expensive-looking wedding ring on her thin finger really told the story. It implied she'd been living a good life. Corinne took a tissue from her purse and clutched it. She seemed almost as nervous as I was uncomfortable.

"So I see Cynthia didn't want to come?" she said.

I shook my head. "No."

"Well..." She sighed. "I guess I deserve that. Lovely, I don't know where to start. So I'll just start off by telling you that I'm not a perfect person. And I've made a lot of mistakes." Corinne raised the tissue then dabbed the corners of her eyes while I looked away—refusing to get emotionally sucked in.

"But I want you to know," she continued, "I never stopped loving you and Cynthia. From a distance, I watched you two grow. I attended both your high school graduations. And—"

"How could you give up your children?" I interrupted.

Corinne shot me a stupefied look. "It wasn't easy, Lovely. You've gotta understand something. I grew up in a very strict, religious household. So when I went away to college, I was young and knew nothing of the world. Then one day on campus, I met Roy Mitchell—a charming handsome musician who took notice of me and my talent. He taught me how to dress, how to sing on stage, and he introduced me to things I had never experienced before. And that's all it took for me to fall in love and get pregnant by a man who was exciting, ambitious but also controlling. By the time we learned Cynthia was on the way, Roy had already convinced me to leave my family, friends, and college education behind to tour with his band. At first, he wanted me to get an abortion—told me we were too close to something big to let a child derail us. But I didn't believe in killing babies. I was already living in sin, not being married to Roy. And killing a child was one sin I couldn't bear to commit. So that's when I decided to reach out to Irene. I'm sure you know that during Irene's freshman year in college, she ran off to Atlantic Beach to elope with a guy named Gavin."

"Yeah, I know about that."

"Well, that didn't make Ms. Dolores happy at all. She showed up on campus so upset and disappointed. But, at the end of the day, she forgave Irene. And that's what I remembered the most—how loving and forgiving Ms. Dolores was. My parents were never like that. So I thought to myself surely Irene's people would take in Cynthia. And that's exactly what they did."

"Roy Mitchell—is he my father too?"

"Yes, of course, Lovely," she said, adamantly. "I was never one to sleep around."

"Is he alive?"

"I'm not sure…haven't seen him in ages."

"You left me on a porch. How could you do that?"

Corinne shook her head. "I'm not proud of that moment. Please believe me when I tell you I had no choice. Roy was absolutely controlling. He made most of the decisions and I depended on him for almost everything. So yet again, he convinced me to give up another child because we were broke and our gigs had dried up. But when he told me to leave you in the hospital bathroom, I just couldn't. Oh, we argued horribly about it. That's when I realized Roy didn't care about anyone except for himself. What a fool I was for thinking he'd marry me after five years of waiting. So I left him. While he slept, I took the car and drove from Tennessee straight to Willisburg. Where else could I go? Not to my parents' house with a newborn baby—that's for sure. But I knew I could count on Irene. Even though she hated my guts, I also knew she would take care of you. So I wrapped you up, put you on the porch and then watched from the bushes as Ms. Dolores rocked you in her arms. You have no idea how hard it was to let you go. The moment you looked into my eyes, I fell in love with you. That's why I named you Lovely."

After hearing that, I almost turned on the water works. But something didn't add up.

"If you loved me and Cynthia so much," I started, "why haven't you tried to contact us all these years? The truth is…if I hadn't approached you at the funeral, we wouldn't be talking right now."

"It's complicated, Lovely. I'm not sure you'd understand."

I gave her a stern look. "Please try me, Ms. Corinne. I'm pretty sharp."

"Like I said, when I returned to South Carolina, I returned with nothing. No degree. No real work experience beyond singing in clubs and no real money. And for a while I tried to make it on my own, but I couldn't. So I had no choice but to go back home and beg for my family's forgiveness. And that's exactly what they made me do—pray day and night on my knees for forgiveness. Then after a few years passed, when they were certain I had repented, my mother arranged for me to meet the son of a prominent pastor with the hope we'd hit it off. Not only was his son a lawyer; he was also a school board member. Well, one year later we married and that made my parents finally proud of me. They told me marrying a God-fearing man like Todd erased my sin of having children out of wedlock and put me back on the path to righteousness."

"Hold on." I smiled sarcastically. "What did they mean by *erased*? Does your husband know you have children?"

Corinne hesitated. "No," she finally answered.

"So that's why you've been avoiding us. You don't want your little secret to get out."

"No, Lovely, that's not it. I really want to have a relationship with you and Cynthia, but I can't tell Todd and Ian about you two right now."

"Ian? Who's Ian?"

"He's your brother."

Wow, this just keeps getting better and better.

I found myself questioning Corinne's motives. "Why did you ask me to come out here? Clearly, you're willing to keep up this charade to protect your family's good name…so why are we here?"

"I guess I deserved that too." She nodded. "Lovely, ever since Ms. Dolores died, I haven't been able to sleep. I keep thinking about how much she's done for me."

"Oh, don't forget about Irene, Aunt Harriet, Uncle Richard, and my father too," I jumped in. "Because together— they all raised us."

"I know. I know," she whimpered. "That's why I'm here today. I just want to say that I am sorry. I'm so sorry for abandoning you and not being a good mother."

Corinne's eyes appeared remorseful, but I saw the whole truth in them. She was a coward—a woman living in fear and hiding behind other people's rules and expectations. I knew she would never find the strength to tell her family about me and Cynthia. She didn't even tell me her married name. I felt sorry for her. For the rest of her life, she would have to suffer with shame, guilt, and secrets. And I knew, all too well from my own experience, that there was healing in telling the truth. But she'd have to discover that on her own.

A sudden peace came over me and then I smiled.

"If you want my forgiveness, then you have it. But I can't promise you a relationship. That takes trust and honesty. But I want to thank you for giving me the best gift ever—my family. You see, they gave me so much love and stability. Not one day did I ever go without."

I stood up feeling satisfied—no longer haunted by curiosity and questions. Cynthia warned me a long time ago that meeting Corinne would leave me disappointed. And she was right, but I felt no hurt. Hurt only comes when love is involved and there was definitely no love here. Corinne remained seated, seemingly in deep thought.

"I'm glad we had a chance to meet. Take care," I said then walked away with no intentions of ever seeing her again.

Chapter 69

October 9, 1998

EVERY morning I did the same thing: jog, shower, step on the scale and then go into Mama's room and cry my eyes out. And today was no different. The scale read 136 pounds— another three pounds down from last week. Mama's room felt empty as usual with no linens on the bed and all of her belongings packed neatly in boxes ready for eventual delivery to the Salvation Army. I sat down on the bed and cried. *Oh, Mama, why did you have to go?*

The seasons were changing. You could feel a hint of coolness in the fall air, yet there were a few fireflies still lingering from summer. Aunt Harriet and I were being lazy rocking in rocking chairs while we enjoyed the light breeze and outside scenery.

"It sure is a fine evening, isn't it Lovely?"

"Yes, ma'am, it is," I replied, watching the mail carrier drive up.

"It's almost 5:30. I wonder why he's so late." I got up and headed for the mailbox.

"Check mine too while you're out there," Aunt Harriet shouted.

I returned to the porch. "You don't have anything," I said, shuffling through letters. But I stopped when I came upon one addressed from Isiah. I opened it.

"You're studying that card mighty hard. Who's it from?" Aunt Harriet asked.

"It's a birthday card from Isiah."

"Ooh, that reminds me," she said excitedly as she lifted herself from the chair. "I've got something for you."

While Aunt Harriet went into the house, I read the card from Isiah.

My Dear Lovely,

I hope this card finds you well. I wanted to wish you a happy birthday, and let you know that I haven't stopped loving you. I think about you daily and hope you will reconsider my invitation one day. There's so much work here for the both of us.

Take care my love, Isiah.

I held the card up to my nose and closed my eyes. I swore I could smell his cologne.

"Here you are." Aunt Harriet came back with a chocolate cupcake decorated with vanilla icing and one lit candle. "Twenty-five years ago you came into our lives on a night just like this. You were a blessing then and you're still a blessing now. Happy birthday, Lovely."

"Aww…thanks, Aunt Harriet. That was sweet. "

"You're welcome, chil'," she said, sitting back down. "Now blow out the candle and make a wish."

After following orders, I gave her a hug and a kiss.

"Lovely, I don't understand. Why aren't you out celebrating your birthday with friends?"

I shrugged. "I'm not sure. Ollie invited me to dinner, but I just don't feel up to it."

"You know Dolores wouldn't want you sitting home."

"I know."

"So what's your friend talking about?" Aunt Harriet pried.

"Oh, he was just wishing me a happy birthday."

"Are you sure that's all? I saw the intensity on your face when I came out here. You were in deep thought."

I sighed. "You're right, Aunt Harriet. There is something else. Isiah wants me to live with him in New York."

"New York City. That sure is a long way from home. So what are you going to do?"

I shook my head. "I don't know. But I do miss him."

"Well, there's your answer."

"What?" I said, surprised. "You think I should go?"

"Don't give me that shocked look. I've been young and in love before. Now, I'm not one to condone shacking up. But if anybody around here deserves some happiness, it's you. So yes, consider the man's offer."

"I just can't leave, Aunt Harriet. I still have obligations— like the house."

"Lovely, what obligations do you have? The house is paid for and willed to you. The only things you have to keep up are the homeowners insurance, property taxes, and utilities. And those can be paid for through the mail. Look honey, you've done your job. There's nothing more for you to do here. So go live your life. The house will be here when you visit."

"What about you? Who'll watch over for you?"

Aunt Harriet chuckled. "Child, I don't need to be watched over. I'll be all right. Besides, I've got Cynthia's number." She stood up. "You think about what I just said. I'm going inside to watch my show."

As I rocked in the chair, listening to crickets and watching fireflies glow green in the air, I thought about Aunt Harriet's words. Maybe it was time to move on. After all, what was holding me back? For my birthday wish, I prayed for direction.

Dear God…I hope I get it.

Chapter 70

THE moment I saw Mrs. Hall through the peephole, I knew Jamal was gone. When I opened the door, she stood at my doorstep in silence. But her red, weary eyes and the urn she held confirmed my intuition. I didn't whoop and holler in pain from the news. The last time I visited Jamal, I just knew it was going to be the last time I'd ever see him alive again.

Mrs. Hall said Jamal passed away about a week ago in a New Orleans hospital from complications from the flu. He arranged for his body to be cremated and then sent home to her. And that was typical of Jamal to do things his way—all the way to the end. But I could only imagine the hurt Mrs. Hall must've felt when she got the call and then the box in the mail. She had no idea her son was sick and back in the hospital.

Mrs. Hall didn't stay long—just long enough for us to weep softly in each other's arms and drop off my portion of Jamal's remains along with a letter. I sat on the couch to prepare myself before reading it. No matter how many times you experience loss, you'll never get used to the emptiness and the gut-stabbing pain it causes.

I felt anxious. *Lovely, just read it!*

Dear Lovely,

If you're reading this letter then I'm already dead. Now stop it! Please, don't cry for me. I have lived my twenty-six years on this earth with love and passion. And I have no regrets. Well, except one. I regret I won't get the chance to walk you down the aisle and give you away to that handsome African man who makes you so happy.

Funny thing about death...the closer you get to it, the wiser you become and begin to see things clearer. For the longest time, you thought you'd never find love. But you did. I believe God loved you enough to keep you away from crap you didn't deserve. And that's why love took its sweet time finding you. But it was worth the wait. You said that yourself. Lovely, you deserve a good man like Isiah. So give love a chance. And as for me, I've had so many loves. But now I see God made you my greatest love of all. And I thank Him so much for that...

I tossed the letter on the coffee table, unable to read the remaining words through my tear-blurred vision. In that moment, it hit me hard that Jamal was really gone. Mama had it right: Tomorrow isn't promised to anyone—neither the young or the old. Now there was just me occupying space in an empty hundred-year-old house, watching it faithfully like a guard dog.

I once asked myself what was holding me back from leaving this town. I think I'd always known the answer—it's me. I spent so much time being devoted to my family; I never learned how to be anything else. Jamal's death was a big sign waving in my face.

I knew what I had to do.

Chapter 71

JAMAL'S memorial service was beautiful and low key, just like he requested. The chapel at the funeral home had bouquets of red roses surrounding Jamal's blown-up portrait and Quincy McNeil played an emotional tribute on his trumpet that even brought the pastor to tears.

Jamal gave me instructions too. In his letter, he asked me to spread his ashes in the ocean at Edisto Beach. He said he wanted to be free and sail the seas just like those loggerhead turtles. I chuckled after reading that because, in some ways, Jamal really did live his life as a loggerhead turtle—determined though unpredictable. But, most importantly…free.

Dressed in jeans and a thick sweater, I stood in the chilly November air to pour Jamal's remains into the ocean. "See you later," I whispered instead of goodbye as they floated away. I no longer believed in goodbyes because I knew I'd see him again—just like I'd see the rest of my family one day in Heaven.

I was back in the car with my suitcases in tow heading for New York to be brave. Jamal said Isiah may be the love of my life. I wasn't too sure of that. But I loved myself enough to give it a shot and finally begin to live.

ACKNOWLEDGMENTS

I'd like to thank so many people for helping me on this project. First, my gratitude goes to God, of course. To my family and friends, thanks for believing in me. To the readers, thanks so much for trusting my work. To Ms. Mary, thanks for your continuous support. And finally, thanks to my editor—Kristen Hamilton.

ABOUT THE AUTHOR

Autumn J. Bright is the author of *Lovely*. Her debut novel, *Love Sick*, was called "searing" by *Publishers Weekly*, and *Kirkus Reviews* magazine listed it as a recommended read. Readers are welcome to learn more about Autumn and future works at www.autumnjbright.com.

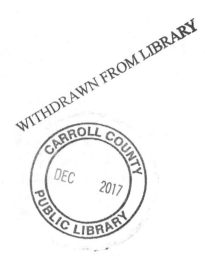
CPSIA information can be obtained
at www.ICGtesting.com
Printed in the USA
LVOW11s2144011117
554606LV00001B/72/P

9 780986 192340